OBLIVION

Henry Clay Childs

ISBN: 1481907506
ISBN 13: 9781481907507

Library of Congress Control Number: 2013906572
CreateSpace Independent Publishing Platform
North Charleston, SC

DEDICATION:

Dedicated to my loving wife, Helen, whose ministrations have made possible all things bright and beautiful in recent times of great stress and challenges. My gratitude transcends the stars, penetrates all dark matter, and is bound by a magic flourish.

CHAPTER ONE

There was so little time. Even less than Avery Lloyd Owens thought as he looked at his watch and cursed. He was late as usual, a habit he had developed happily as a lad growing up in rural Wales. But this time he could at least blame his frustration on the traffic up Whitehall that had his cabbie fuming as well.

London cabdrivers, he knew, were renowned for their sangfroid in the worst of times. Their brains had even been proven to expand and contract as need dictated. The memory portion expanded, since a comfortable knowledge of every conceivable address in the city had to be part of their litany. And some obscure part of the brain had to curtail the need for pit stops.

The last thing Avery needed to think about at the moment was the whereabouts of the nearest men's room, or lavatory, as he still called them. He had never been able to conquer the simple reflex response: the need to go once the thought occurred to him. Not even now as he was trying to get to the Royal Society of Astronomers to deliver his latest findings on the evolution of the universe.

The extravagant statue of General Sir Douglas Haig on horseback loomed above him in the centre of the broad avenue that led up to Trafalgar Square from the Palace of Westminster. Avery had to suppress the urge to ask his cabbie to wait for him while he used the base of the statue as a pissoir. Pinching himself, he knew the impulse was as tribal as it was visceral, for there were few men, he was sure, who were born and bred in Wales who wouldn't take delight, albeit possibly childish, in pissing all over the relics of the old empire. And that statue was a prime example of the puffery that once stood for grandeur across much of the British Empire.

"Whatever in bloody hell do you think is holding us up, driver?" He flinched since he knew anger never helped in a situation like this.

"Just a little demonstration, gov'nor." The cabbie's grey eyes focused briefly on Avery in the rear-view mirror. His dark eyebrows, as bushy as his moustache, seemed to contain as much potential for hurling lightning bolts as any Olympian god's. "Little buggers who want us to get out of Afghanistan, I do believe."

"Well, now, do I detect a believer in the theory that we should all be the Yanks' poodle?" Avery watched the reaction to this question with particular curiosity.

"Beggin' your lordship's pardon, but I am of an age that can remember when our bulldog very much needed the Yankee poodle to help in that minor scrape with ol' Adolph and Co." A quick brush to his moustache accentuated the intensity of his feeling.

"Fair enough, my man." Avery had to concentrate on fashioning an answer and was relieved to find his need to desecrate imperial memories was fast declining. "I won't even argue that the thoroughly evil traffickers in drugs that are dulling the wits of much of our youth are remotely on a par with Hitler."

"Certainly not yet, gov. But maybe we just need to wait a while. My daughter is one of those up ahead making my day longer and your patience shorter, and there isn't a thing I can do or say that makes the slightest difference to her, one way or t'other."

Avery sat back with a twinge of relief. "You poor bastard" was all he could manage to mutter, thankful that he had never had any children.

"You can say that again, gov. Me missus calls me that all the time now…and shakes her head at the very thought that we brought the poor wretch into the world in the first place." He shook his shaggy head. "We both thank our lucky stars that we only have the one to contend with, you know?" His eyes searched for understanding in the mirror, a hint of remorse briefly clouding them. "Ah!" Traffic began to move again, and both men felt the stress of the moment begin to ebb.

Several minutes later, safely delivered to the Royal Society's door, Avery lifted his eyes to the inscription over the entrance. *"Ad astra, per scientia."* His immediate impulse was to raise his hand in greeting. Self-consciously, he abbreviated the move chest high and stifled the royal wave he enjoyed affecting as the doorman eyed him with what vaguely resembled amusement. "A bee sting," he muttered unnecessarily as he bowed in gratitude for the opened door.

"Quite, sir. Welcome back to the Royal Society." The hint of a smile on the doorman's face was as likely the by-product of familiarity as of simple amusement.

Avery shed his raincoat as he strode to the cloak room to the right of the marble-floored and musty hall that welcomed the more quizzical minds of Britain on a monthly basis. Nodding to the small clusters of wool-wearing members, most of whom he knew, he ducked into the gents with a sigh of relief. He chose not to take note of the similar looks of bemusement on many of the faces that followed his progress. "Familiarity," he muttered as he unzipped his fly. "The bane of many an existence."

Hands washed and a smile smoothly etched, he swung wide the door and had to suppress yet another urge—one to bow and doff an imaginary plumed hat worthy of Cyrano de Bergerac. "Gentlemen," he began, favouring his lower back. "I do believe we have a fair pickle of a conundrum on our hands this day."

"We thought we might be able to count on you, Owens, to spice up our day, one way or another." This from a jolly-faced, bespectacled older chap who obviously had the respect of all there gathered.

"My dear Watson, I knew I could count on you to keep an open mind, at least as long as the spices hold up." Avery found himself pounding his colleague on the back with such vigour that the latter looked quite startled. "Humble apologies, dear chap. I just have such a sense as to how things might be going…that is to say, 'how things went,' that my anterior tibia couldn't hold back."

"Anterior tibia? Do you mean to say…?" A much younger man took a tentative step forward. Owens had never seen him before. "Are you implying that you have a leg sticking out of your…?"

"My arse? Certainly nothing of the sort. Just a little bit of scientific slobbering that we indulge in here from time to time." Avery looked at the gathering group and raised his eyebrows expectantly.

"Oh, sorry, Owens. This is Derwentwater. Damien Derwentwater. He's here on probation for the month." Watson's eyes rolled with restrained disapproval.

"New College, Oxford, sir." The young man offered a hand. "Sorry to be so obtuse."

"My dear fellow, it is we who are obtuse…or at least we make a game stab at it." Avery accepted the firm handshake and made a quick assessment of the handsome face. With a smile firmly back in place, he lifted his sheaf of papers and nodded toward the auditorium door. "Shall we venture forth then, gentlemen, over the rainbow and beyond the known galaxies?"

Twenty minutes later, as the last stragglers settled into their uncomfortable wooden seats, Avery took a last sip of water and squinted out at the assembled crowd. His weathered face, cloaked in a fine, greying beard, clipped short, fairly sparkled with anticipation. "Gentlemen," he began and then reared back in surprise at the sight of two ladies toward the back. "And ladies…this is a rare treat."

Several heads turned to note the distaff among them, a few finding it difficult to conceal their displeasure.

Avery shook his head and tugged briefly at his beard. "You will note, dear colleagues, that I have no slides to dazzle you with, no images of nebulae or pulsars or even white dwarfs." He lowered his glasses and acknowledged the general discomfort he knew was being felt. Children, he thought with some amusement, they need elemental entertainment, or are forever lost in space. A smile erupted at that thought, and he made a show of arranging his papers.

"The reason for the lack of special effects is simple. In the past several months, we have witnessed the findings of several of our esteemed colleagues, who have illustrated the tantalizing evidence that there is much more 'up there' that not only doesn't meet the eye but penetrates to the reptilian brain we inherited from our earliest ancestors."

The inevitable stir swirled around the room, much to Avery's amusement. His eyes briefly settled on the two ladies, who were huddled together in a most animated conversation, albeit behind gloved hands. "The growing evidence," he continued, "that there is such a major role to be played by what we call 'dark matter' and now 'dark energy' virtually precludes the need for images. Indeed, the use of images clouds our ability to fully

4

understand the nature of what we have to deal with." There was more stir and more animated exchange between the two ladies and more discomfort shown by many of the older members of the audience.

"See here, Owens, you're not trying to sell us that poppycock notion of yours again that the invisible is more important than what we can observe and measure." This from one of Avery's least favourite colleagues, an Englishman to the wrong manner borne.

"My dear Higgins, I have not yet begun to fight, as a fellow Welshman was once quoted as saying." Avery took special glee at annoying this man and almost regretted that his beard concealed a good bit of his pleasure. He swept a hand through his thinning locks, strands that tended to grow straight back from his high forehead. He then gripped the podium with both hands and braced for the criticism he knew awaited. At five foot ten, he didn't offer an imposing figure up there, he knew, even though his years as a scratch golfer had kept him in fine shape.

"What the world faces today is unlike any challenge that we may have known in the past." His mind briefly conjured up the image of Haig's statue. It was the perfect example of misguided values. Haig had been the supreme commander of the forces at the Battle of the Somme, the First World War's most devastating loss of life, particularly on the Allied side. How could a nation honour such a man, such a tragedy? He shook his head, scouring the audience for any supportive faces and once again found himself admiring the intelligent, sensitive faces of the two ladies.

"We have survived two world wars, several incompetent leaders, in a myriad of disciplines…even the Norman invasion." His face crinkled at the brief self-indulgent chuckle that rippled around the room. "But what we face today"—he raised a hand with forefinger vaguely resembling God's in Michelangelo's *Creation of Man*—"is far more insidious, as it is totally beyond our ken, totally beyond our ability to"—he gestured to Higgins—"measure and observe."

More sounds of discomfort and shuffling of feet.

"Excuse me, sir, but what is it that you are referring to?" This from one of the ladies. "My friend and I are new to your club and—"

"We are not a club, my dear lady. We are the Royal Society of Astronomers. Dear lord, save us from ignorance!" This from yet another older member, whose eyes rolled in disbelief.

"I beg your pardon, sir. Not a club, of course…a royal society. Quite. But we are still in need of some explanation as to what—"

"Of course. Of course. You are not alone, I can assure you." Avery adjusted his glasses and gazed around the room at the general air of discomfort and uncertainty everywhere. "But to address your immediate question, may I briefly recount the findings that we as a club…as a Society…have determined thus far?" He paused. "Will the assembly allow a brief recap of our findings?"

As there were no objections, Avery waved his hand as though holding a magic wand, slowly assembled his thoughts and cleared his throat. "In the Beginning, dear ladies, it was postulated that there was nothing but potential, nothing but a single tiny dot of energy, that through some miraculous bit of mischief gave rise to the Big Bang." He paused to note whatever looks of disapproval might have cropped up around the room. Seeing only the usual culprits, he continued.

"Now the bible says that there was at least something more substantial than the essential nothing from whence the Big Bang emerged. The ancient Israelites assumed—I believe I can use such a word—that there was what they refer to as 'the Word.'" He waved a dismissive hand. "That has given me the satisfaction of assuming that there was at least a great deal of gas at the Beginning"—the sound of subdued moans of disapproval and mockery stirred the sultry air— "from whence the many millions of words that have ensued over the centuries initially sprang."

More sounds of disapproval only encouraged Avery to warm to his subject. "But, my dear ladies, you may share my scepticism at even such a brave interpretation of Creation. God, after all, or 'The Creator,' as I would have it, would need more than just gas to create all that we know, much less all that we do *not* know." He smiled at the restless sense of tension that was building.

"All of which brings us to the crux of your enquiry. 'What is it that we do not know?' And the answer to that is conveniently summed up in the expression 'dark matter.' That, by definition, is what we believe to exist but that we cannot, currently, take the measure of."

The ladies both nodded, as though they understood, or at least were grateful for the explanation that, of course, fell woefully short of satisfaction.

"Are you going to continue to beat a dead horse here, Owens? Or are you going to tell us something that is worth putting off lunch for?" This came from yet another protagonist of the English persuasion.

"Dangling participles, are we, Wooster? Heaven forefend that I keep you from your appointed rounds." Avery patted his own slightly protruding belly and brought a guffaw or two from the crowd. Holding up both hands by way of a partial retreat and partial entreaty, he continued. "I shall make this as brief and indelible as possible. It has come to my attention that all the evidence that we have at our disposal in fact points to the high improbability of a Big Bang starting off the festivities that we know as the universe. Quite the contrary. The presence of the dark energy and dark matter we all—or almost all—have come to accept as fact virtually precludes any possible existence of nothing before all hell broke loose."

"Poppycock!"

"Get your wicked self back to Wales!"

"What a disgrace to our hallowed halls of science, our history of discovery, our very British bones!"

These and other *cries de coeur* sounded around the auditorium. And Avery relished every anguished sound.

CHAPTER TWO

The two ladies were waiting in the front hall just as Avery had hoped they might. There were plenty of others, mostly red faced and fit to be tied, but he managed to ignore them as he made his way to where the ladies stood expectantly.

"Sorry to expose you to such old-world reactionaries, but I suppose this is where you are liable to find more of them than anywhere this side of the nearest graveyard." He bowed and extended a hand to each, happy to have managed a slight flourish of his sword hand were he his hero, Cyrano de Bergerac.

"A most interesting theory, Mr. Owens, or should I say lack of one?" The taller of the two young ladies, dark of hair and keen of eye, allowed a slight smile to warm her otherwise stern features.

Avery shrugged and waved his hands in a sign of resignation. "There is just too much to process yet. But, as I was able to make clear, I hope"—he bowed to both of his audience—"there is far too much that cannot be ignored, given the evidence that is coming in at a frightening rate nowadays."

"I thought you to be particularly brave in mentioning the possible link, biblically speaking, between your dark matter and the Prince of Darkness." The shorter of the two ladies, reddish blonde hair cascading down her shoulders, looked up at Avery with a sprightly twinkle in her striking green eyes.

"Ah, ah! Not *my* dark matter, Miss…"

"Fairfax. Fiona Fairfax, at your service." The young lady gave a version of a curtsey as she held Avery's admiring gaze steadily. He realized she would be quite attractive but for a broken nose. That aquiline feature zigged at an almost comical angle. Her deep, husky voice suggested not only a keen preference for whiskey but possibly an accompanying stogie as well.

"Yes, Miss Fairfax—indeed a pleasure." He bowed since he hoped to identify the fragrance that wafted from her shoulders. "As I must make clear, this whole business of dark matter is hardly of my making—if you will pardon the blasphemy." He smiled as both ladies broke into laughter. "But the idea that we are getting close to discovering the true makeup of the universe and all its constituent parts, including what we have so derisively termed 'social issues,' makes for many a sleepless night, at least for me."

"You poor soul." The dark-haired one reached out to touch Avery's elbow. "Sleep deprivation is always such a drain on one's energy. At least that is what I have always experienced." She winked, and Avery felt as though he were falling under a spell he could not quite comprehend.

"You have the advantage of me, dear lady." Avery raised both wiry eyebrows in expectation.

"People call me Missy, Mr. Owens. My parents named me Quentin Elisabeth, which really did me little good in school, somehow." She shook her head. "Quentin Elisabeth Demarest. Can you imagine a more unkind fate as a child?"

"Why, certainly I can. There are a raft of names that come to mind that—"

"My dear Mr. Owens, you quite miss the point. My initials are—"

"Of course. Q.E.D. How silly of me. *Quod erat demonstrandum*—'As it has been proven.' My favourite expression in Latin. So you wound up with variations on rodents and toads, I suspect, if your peers were anywhere near as mean minded as my school chums."

"Very good, Mr. Owens." She gave him a look that felt to him very much like a CAT scan.

"Do call me Avery, would you? I feel quite old enough as it is without being addressed as though I had one foot in the hereafter."

9

"But we both thought that, from your talk, you quite understood that that was your vantage point...your advanced stage of life." Fiona gave him a mock smile that sent a slight shiver up his spine.

Avery began to feel a bit outmanoeuvred just standing there. As fate would have it, Higgins interrupted.

"I say there, old man, have you totally lost all the sawdust that God tried to stuff into that cranium of yours?" Higgins puffed out his chest as he bowed to the two ladies, whose attention he obviously relished. "Aren't you going to introduce me, Owens?"

"I don't believe you need much of an introduction, Higgins, but this is Miss Fairfax and Miss Demarest." The two made a totally fraudulent effort to impress him, a fact hopelessly lost on the man as he eyed each with the manner of a hungry crocodile gliding toward unsuspecting gazelles.

An embarrassing silence followed, broken by the appearance of the young Oxonian, Derwentwater. Both young ladies appreciated his cautious look.

"Ah, here is some new blood, ladies, infused into the old arteries of our organization." Avery introduced the lad with an air of relief as Higgins took the hint and backed away. "So what do you think of the can of worms I just opened up for all to contemplate, eh, Derwentwater? The ladies here think there might be a glimmer of truth or, should I say, possibility? in what I sense is around the corner." Avery eyed the young man with the same intensity as did the ladies.

"Well, sir, I must admit to coming from a region—the borders, as doubtless you know—where we hold that all things are possible." He looked expectantly at each of the three, his dark eyes searching for under-standing and acceptance.

"Of course!" Fiona raised a delicate hand to point at Derwentwater's chin. "I went to school with one of your cousins, unless I am very much mistaken. Hilary, from the East Riding? Very interesting girl."

"Yes. How odd you should have known Hilary. We do miss her terribly, after all." Derwentwater tried unsuccessfully to contain a frown and look of deep sadness.

"Whatever did happen to the poor girl?" Fiona's voice had the hollow ring of certainty.

"Why, she just disappeared." His eyes widened in disbelief. "After going off to that...strange school—not yours, I'm sure—she seemed to become another person entirely. Very…fey, I would like to think, though her parents were convinced that she had been drugged and brainwashed." He looked helplessly at Fiona for understanding.

"Surely not drugs and all that foolishness about the Jonestown syndrome. Not here in England." Missy turned to stare at her friend as though she were reading her mind.

"Not even in the border country, I suspect. I'm sure she is quite happy, wherever she might be, you know, Mr. Derwentwater." This with unusual certainty from Missy.

"Do call me Damien, please. I am the seventh earl, but in this day and age, 'Lord Damien' does seem a bit out of place, don't you think?"

"In any day and age, if you ask me" Fiona blurted out even as she reconfigured her features into a radiant smile.

"The seventh, you say," Avery broke in, back from a reverie that had intruded unbidden. "That would put the first somewhere in the time of…"

"George the Third." Damien flashed a brief, uncertain smile. "Our mad king." His smooth features gave him the appearance of being in his early thirties. A strong chin and prominent aquiline nose gave him the appearance to match his pedigree.

"Goodness, you lot are a slow bunch of breeders," Avery said. "Seven generations in—let me see—two hundred fifty odd years. That is quite an arithmetic accomplishment." All eyes turned to study Damien's reaction.

"A mere thirty or so years per generation, actually. We Derwentwaters are known to be a bit on the hesitant side when it comes to such matters as marriage and…" His voice trailed off.

"And schooling, Master Damien?" This from a bemused Fiona.

"Well, quite!" He hesitated. "There has always been an interest in what Mr. Owens has described as 'the can of worms' theory in our family, to be quite honest. It has brought grief on many a generation, I am sorry to say. The neighbours," he continued, "even went so far as to burn down our home some three hundred years ago—a very nice little spot built back in 1482. Just because of a bit of wizardry." He shook his head. "Great loss, that."

"A great condemnation of your neighbours, I would say." Both ladies nodded vigorously at that comment from Avery. "Well, I would say that we are well met, then. We may be the only ones here who have sufficiently open minds to contemplate the turning of the worm, so shall we retire to the nearest pub to further explore the possibilities?"

"Oh," said the ladies simultaneously. "We know just the spot."

The atmosphere at the Goat and Dragon Pub, just blocks from the Society's prim neighbourhood, was full of indefinable energy. The assemblage appeared to be your average collection of London's bohemian set, and yet there was something about the way many watched the entrance of the newly formed foursome that caught Avery's attention. A knowing smile, almost a smirk, appeared on many of the upturned faces as they passed.

"Funny how I never knew of this place before," he half-muttered to himself. Fiona turned to give him a pitying glance. "Seems nice enough, of course," he added quickly. "You two come here often?"

"Oh, every once in a while, I suppose" was Missy's casual answer.

"Whenever the spirit moves us," Fiona added with a deep guttural laugh.

They found a table toward the back to accommodate the four of them and quickly ordered pints for the men and daiquiris for the ladies. "Well, Damien, do tell us more about that brush with wizardry your family had way back when." Avery voiced the question they all were interested to have answered.

"Well, I'm not sure that I really can. All that I ever learned was the hearsay that comes down through the centuries, you know." He cleared his throat and tried to gather his thoughts, as dispersed by time as they were. "My great-great-great-grandmother was a Scot from just across the border or 'above the wall,' as we say."

"Hadrian's Wall, is that?" Fiona couldn't help herself.

"Aye, lass." Damien was seemingly unaware that he had lapsed into a Scottish brogue. "Frae the borders. An Armstrong, do ye ken? A sheep-stealing race of fine, upstanding folk."

Everyone found amusement at this seeming incongruity. "And, as you know"—his voice returned to a less-distinctive northern accent—"the Scots are a superstitious people, blessed with the imagination of a Tolkien, crossed with the memory of a Homer. It was this simple, smouldering concoction that brought about the natural curiosity in 'the other side,' as we call the afterlife. And the most ready access to that other side lay in certain concoctions and incantations now long lost, I'm sorry to say." He smiled apologetically and shrugged.

"Oh, I wouldn't be so certain that they are all lost, my dear Damien." Fiona laid a hand gently on his sleeve as the drinks were delivered and everyone ducked to one side or the other to avoid being struck by the rough manner of the waiter. "Missy and I have made an effort over the past few years to retrieve what we could of ancient…practices and have been quite surprised at the amount of findings still lingering."

"England and, one might say, all of Britain is, after all, the home of much of what the outside world would label as sorcery, even to this day." Missy's smooth, pale features seemed to tense into odd wrinkles as she glanced proudly around the table.

Avery couldn't help but chime in. "I remember my mother telling me, with the straightest of faces and even the stiffest of backs, that the Nazi invasion was repelled by dint of the white witches of Britain getting together to cast a spell on Hitler."

"Not just the white ones, from what I was told." Missy seemed upset that she had let that out without proper editing. As a cover she raised her glass and intoned "To new friendships, old concepts, and future conquests."

All raised their glasses, and Avery thought he heard Fiona mutter something about "old devil rum," but the sound of laughter from a neighbouring table drowned out any certainty.

"Well," Avery began with some hesitation, "I am most curious to hear what you all think of the probable role that dark matter plays in our lives—in the existence of the universe."

Silence fell as each of the three looked at the others to start the conversation. Finally, after a careful draft of her drink, Fiona spoke. "I, for one, am relieved to find that such a concept is finally on the table." She shot a stern look of certainty at Missy, who nodded in quiet concurrence. "For those of us who, like Damien's family, have an interest in the occult, the inclusion of dark matter as a 'constituent part' of things, as you so aptly put it, Avery, has long been a given."

Missy quickly chimed in. "There is no conceivable explanation for how things are without including dark matter as an essential ingredient in the makeup of what we know as life."

Avery just shook his head at this obvious truth that had escaped him for so long.

Damien chose to add a measure of emphasis. "One thing that has always been clear to my family is that the biblical partition of the world into light and darkness holds true." He threw up his hands. "If there were no dichotomy, then how might a religious person explain the Holocaust or AIDS or any of the apparent desecrations that have plagued humanity since the beginning of time?"

Avery struck his mug with unintended force on the already battered table. "Why was it, Damien, that you said 'apparent desecrations'? How odd that you should qualify the despicable acts of history like that!"

Damien winced and lowered his gaze. "I have no idea why I said that." His eyes rose to scrutinize each of the three at the table. "But somewhere in my head I felt a doubt about the judgment of history." He held a delicate hand up to his sweating forehead.

"Interesting, my dear chap." Avery watched as the two ladies reached to console the young man. "It would seem that the dark matter is manifesting itself right here at our table. But…there is no physical reaction to its presence if, indeed, it is here. And all the laws of physics that *I* know of dictate that the known, visible elements demonstrate through gravitational abnormalities the presence of dark matter." He looked around and made a comical effort to discover something under the table, inadvertently glancing at the attractive sight of the ladies' exposed legs.

"My dear Avery, are you just a dirty old man in astronomer's clothing?" Missy gave a tug at her skirt even as she threw her head back in mock amusement.

A loud curse sounded from surprisingly close by. "You lecherous old bugger! What are you doing looking up the skirt of this fair damsel?" A tall, teetering figure loomed behind Missy.

"Now, Willy, this is no time to be like that." Missy half-turned to confront the already seething figure. "Calm down, I say, Willy, or I will have to take measures."

This threat seemed to have an immediate effect, much as a slap in the face might have. The intruder took a half step back and wiped his mouth with the back of his hand. "Are you sure now, Missy? Are you true sure?"

"Quite sure, Willy. Now get along home and stop scaring our new friends." Missy grimaced in real displeasure and shooed her stalwart guardian away. "I do apologize. Willy means well, he really does. He is just too fond of me, I fear, and will go off the handle at the least thought of a slight." She shook her head with a vague air of contentment. "I had no idea that he was even there. Now that is how excited I am about our little group."

Avery watched the retreating figure that had just broken into their burgeoning circle. "Odd sort of chap, isn't he?"

"But quite special, really. William Drury Hamilton had quite a life before...losing it." Missy gave Fiona a knowing glare.

"Hamilton? A Scot?" Damien eyed the departing soul with new interest.

"By way of Bournemouth on his mother's side. A bit diluted, I fear." Fiona took another sip of her drink.

"And as besotted as too many of our brethren these days, from the look of things," Damien added.

"Well, as I said, he has had a number of challenges in his life and for some unknown reason has latched onto us as surrogate sisters, or some such relationship." Missy pulled at her delicately carved chin and left a slight trail of red on her alabaster skin.

Avery took in all of this with a quiet sense of comprehension. He could feel a tension in the air that belied the general spirit of frivolity—and alcohol-driven escapism—that permeated the pub. He tried to take in whatever elements that came into play: the two ladies at his table, who seemed to be known by most there; the strange outburst of anger by the tipsy Mr. Hamilton; the sense of—that was it—the sense of community, though stronger, a sense of kinship more than anything appeared to pulsate through the room. Excluding him and Damien, of course. It was quite fascinating and certainly not unknown in British pubs everywhere, but somehow different.

"Well, Damien, what are your thoughts, now that we are free of Mr. Hamilton's surveillance, on the topic at hand?" Avery leaned forward with a squint and a bemused smile.

"Well, sir, I am reminded of such chaps as that Aleister Crowley fellow who took up residence by Loch Ness some hundred years ago and apparently conjured up some spirits that he failed to dispatch back to the nether regions, leaving them to haunt his home to this day." He raised his slender eyebrows in dismay.

"Oh, him!" Fiona fairly twisted out of her chair. "That fable is so totally debunked I can't believe that you would cite it, Damien."

"Debunked by whom, my dear Fiona?" Damien sat back with the air of some authority. "I have spoken to more than one individual who has ventured by the house in question and heard some most harrowing tales."

"By superstitious Scotsmen, I suspect," Fiona flung back.

"By those poor, susceptible souls surely but by a Yank or two as well." He paused only briefly. "And we all know full well that our American friends are not prone to flights of fancy when it comes to ghosts and spirits and the like."

"Far too bull-headed, aren't they?" agreed Missy.

"Or pragmatic, as I believe they would say," added Avery.

"I sometimes wonder if they are capable of seeing ghosts, what with their particular genetic makeup, you know?" Fiona flirted with Damien for a moment.

"I hate to admit that the very same thought has occurred to me." Damien broke out laughing.. "It would seem that our fey manner and... general background make us far more capable of...acknowledging things and...understanding matters that others just cannot."

"Matters such as the dark stuff?" injected Avery.

"Very possibly, yes." Damien knitted his brow. "I had never thought it through quite like that before, but, of course, that would seem to be a natural consequence. National sensitivity need not be a national obsession, however." He held up a cautionary hand with the shadow of a frown.

"Of course not." Missy gave him a friendly tap on the arm. "But it does give us a possible real advantage in understanding what Mr. Owens has postulated—an advantage that few others may be able to duplicate."

Avery didn't bother to plead for a less formal form of address as he leaned in to draw his followers into a close scrum of conspiracy over the centre of the table. "If we can just conjure up the necessary...skills to help decipher what the dark matter really means and how it is applied to life as we know it...then we might be on to something worth a true celebration."

"We could even include Willy in on the fireworks," exclaimed Fiona with delight.

"I wouldn't want to go quite that far," Damien began. "But—"

"Oh, Willy is a far more reasonable person when he is sober, and... he has certain skills that we might find helpful." Missy raised her carefully drawn eyebrows with a mysteriously sly expression.

"I can't wait to learn what those skills might be," said Damien. "He did remind me, now that I think of it, a bit of Boris Karloff hamming it up as a member of the undead."

"Damien! Really! What a terrible thing to say!" Fiona couldn't conceal a slight smile as she tried to feign indignation. "We really need to keep our wits about us if we are going to decipher the powers that may well lurk in this mysterious realm that Avery has brought to our attention."

The two men exchanged glances that clearly indicated they were the ones who needed to catch up with what the ladies seemed already to know. The uncertainty made Avery's brain seem to overheat from the exertion, bringing a new dimension of reality into play that he had never felt before. It hurt.

"What say we have another round and try to pin down some of the basics we are dealing with. Sound good?" Avery put a hand to his head and just had to hope that another drink might clear his mind of whatever force had begun to seep into it.

"I'm ready," Fiona croaked as she finished off the remainder of her drink. Damien and Missy agreed, and the ritual of dodging the waiter's efforts at delivery soon followed.

CHAPTER THREE

Willy Hamilton took a swipe at the cat as he barged through the door of his mother's flat. With a yowl that was pure disdain, the cat dodged the foot and clambered up a nearby bookcase. Peering down with intense brown eyes, it followed Willy's stumbling progress as though from memory. Implacable thoughts spun through its head.

"Hey, Mother, where did you hide the detox potion?" Willy grabbed his head to make sure it hadn't fallen from his shoulders.

"Where it's always been, you numbskull." The disembodied voice sounded as though from the fifth circle of hell. "In the toolbox your father left before he…departed."

"Departed? You mean shot himself? Is that what you mean?" Willy hated the way his mother glossed over the big things in life.

"Whatever."

He hated that, too. The adoption by a ninety-two-year-old woman of one of the more inane expressions of the young. Her shadow somehow appeared just ahead of his progress toward the life-saving toolbox, and he glanced over his shoulder to be certain she wasn't up to her usual tricks. There she stood, all four foot ten inches of pure venom masquerading as an old hag. Even her long, drooping nose came from central casting.

"You got some real reason for that elixir, Son? You know that it only lasts for so long, like everything else, before the effect don't work no more." Her accent was of the south coastal region.

Willy brought himself up short. His dazed expression gave little indication of the concentration he was trying to give to his mother's point. "Well, damnation. I just thought a little…well, damnation…"

"That's it, Son. You just give some real thought to what you want to become, you hear?" Her voice sounded a lot like Fiona's, only with the cackle of old age. "You keep taking refuge in that old concoction, and one day you'll just turn into a toad, and that will be that." She eyed the cat. "Euripides will tear your head off and swallow your entrails for breakfast."

Willy eyed the cat with renewed dislike. "If that bleeding little bugger comes near me again, it will pay with a free ticket through the window. This right foot o' mine used to be able to send a bundle of those damned things through a goalpost at forty yards." He swung his foot loosely and pointed at the cat, who hissed at him savagely.

"If you don't mind your manners, boy, there is going to be all hell breaking loose, and I don't know if I'm going to be able to put the devil back in the bottle, if you catch my meaning." She squinted first at her son and then at the cat, and turned to leave.

"Sure, Mother. I know what you mean. I'm not a complete moron."

"That's a relief to hear!" This from the next room.

Willy took one more step toward the toolbox and noticed that Euripides half-crouched in what had to be joyous anticipation. That did it. Anything to piss off the cat. He turned and went instead to the icebox for some vegetable juice.

* * *

Back at the Goat and Dragon, Avery was wishing he hadn't ordered another pint. Normally he could down three or four without thinking, but this time was quite different. He lowered his mug as carefully as he could and tried to concentrate on the conversation that was getting increasingly animated, even without him.

"If we can assume that there is a correlation between dark matter and the spirit world, that should make any insights far easier." Damien.grunted absent-mindedly.

"But we don't need insights," countered Fiona. "We need to establish the relationship between the spirit world and the vast amount of dark matter that Avery says exists…that is to say, that he says that others say exist."

All Avery could do was nod and look to Missy to add her observations.

"I have to admit that I am amazed that someone has calculated that dark matter comprises so much of the universe." Missy seemed quite buoyant. "I always felt that there was a basic balance between…dark and light, good and evil. This comes as a major surprise, I must say."

"What we need to do is try and determine if there is a causal effect, you know?" Damien was on the verge of something.

Missy raised a slender hand and pointed skyward. "Just what I was thinking. If there is so much dark matter out there and only so much evil, there may not be a direct correlation after all."

Avery turned to confront Missy. "Don't forget that there is supposed to be a simple relationship between the dark stuff and what we can observe—the so-called good stuff. Or am I complicating matters?" He shook his head and wished he had remained silent.

"There is no question but that we don't know anything concrete— what a word—about any of this, so…" Fiona gave a knowing glance at Missy. "We need to consult an expert."

Damien seemed to read their minds. "Willy?"

"No, not Willy so much as his mother." Missy raised an eyebrow as though speaking of an august being.

"Of course." Fiona clapped her hands in conspiratorial agreement. "Old Betty from Bournemouth is one of the best…experts there is on what we need to know!"

Avery and Damien exchanged chagrined glances at being so out of touch. "Is this lady widely known?" Avery raised a tired eyebrow.

"Good lord, yes. Or, rather, no. Not *widely* known. Just to a few of us, I suppose. And she is no lady." Fiona fairly guffawed at the thought.

Missy nodded, trying to keep a straight face. "About as far from being a lady as she can get, I suspect."

Again the men exchanged glances. Avery remained in the dark, but Damien was catching on. "So, we have a true practitioner of the "ancient arts," do we?"

"One of the best!" Fiona's bright green eyes widened with glee. "If anyone can help us understand the relationship between dark matter and… the old ways, it should be Betty."

"*If* there is a relationship," interrupted Damien.

Avery winced, as though from some childhood memory. "Good boy, Damien. There always needs to be a sceptic when venturing into foreign waters. And for my money, this sounds more like extraterrestrial waters than anything else."

"Not really, you know." Missy laid a hand on Avery's as it clung to his mug. "You astronomers should always cock an eye toward your brethren's discipline, astrology. It would make your life infinitely more compelling, you know."

"I have been told that on more than one occasion, actually." Avery briefly recalled a gorgeous creature who had called herself Andromeda. Talk about celestial bodies. He had been far too shy to allow her into his narrow orbit of existence in those early years and had paid the price in remorse ever since. Now the price was about to skyrocket, he noted with a tug of a smile beneath his beard.

"What is it that we have to do to consult with this 'Betty from Bournemouth'? Ring a bell? Snuff a candle?" Avery began to feel life returning to his outer limbs.

"Very funny! No, nothing quite so prosaic, I can assure you. But…" Fiona's voice trailed off.

"But there might be a bit of indoctrination that you two will have to go through," concluded Missy.

Damien's face contorted. "Ugh. You mean, bite the head off a bat? Eat scorpions whole? That sort of thing?"

Fiona frowned, then contorted her face into a broad smile. Her broken nose seemed to straighten with the transformation. "What a great idea, Damien! I will be sure to pick up some scorpions on the way over. There's an ever-so-nice shop just around the corner from where she lives."

Both men felt queasy at the thought, even though they were certain that Fiona was only joking. "How convenient," Damien managed.

"Well, it is clear that you two need some indoctrination into the ways of…dark matters, so I suspect that we should get on with it." Missy pushed back her chair. "What do you think, Fiona, dear? Are these two remotely ready?"

Fiona's chair made an odd screaming sound as it was pushed back. "We shall soon see, shan't we?"

Minutes later, without any stop offs, much to the men's relief, they were knocking on the door of an oddly abandoned-looking building of three stories with filthy windows and peeling paint.

"Are you sure this is where the lady of Bournemouth dwells?" Avery's hand rested on the metal railing, and he felt the rust come off beneath his grasp.

"Oh, quite, dear sir." Fiona had become quite tense as they stood waiting. "And she is no lady, as you will soon see."

The front door opened a crack, and Willy's tousled head could be seen studying the situation. Suddenly the door was flung open, and the tall figure lunged forward to give Missy an awkward hug. "Are ye all right, lassie? They have done you no harm, I trust." He glared at Avery and Damien as though they were hounds from hell.

"Everything is fine, Willy. We are here to see your mother, if she will allow it." Missy broke away from his grasp.

"Mother? You want to see *my* mother?" He was quite perplexed at that. He stepped back to allow the four to enter the dingy foyer, still hung over from his visit to the pub. Making a vain effort to straighten his thick, dark hair, he gestured for all to climb the stairs. "She will be on the third floor by now, preparing for a check on the position of certain stars."

"Aha! A fellow astronomer, is she?" Avery felt somehow uncomfortable saying this.

"Hardly" was Willy's curt reply. "Just checking for some conjunctions, if you know what I mean."

"Of course. Of course, I'm sure we all understand what you mean there, Willy…er, Mr. Hamilton." Avery nudged Damien as they climbed past various piles of trash along the stairwell.

Willy glowered at Missy, then turned back to address Avery. "'Willy' will do. Mr. Hamilton is long dead, and I have no wish to wind up as he did."

No one has any immediate reaction to that comment. Feeling the stress of climbing three flights of creaky stairs kept the group quiet until they reached the top landing. "Good exercise, what?" Damien broke the silence with an effort to appear less than winded.

"I often think that mother floats up these stairs while I grunt and sweat," Willy added with an unexpected effort at humour.

"This is a great argument for levitation, I must say," Avery added, puffing away.

The ladies seemed least affected and most anxious to push on through the heavy metal door to the rooftop. Willy signalled for them to wait as he tentatively poked his head outside. "Mother, we have visitors. Is it all right to bring them on out?"

"Of course, you fool. I have been expecting them, after all, even the one who claims to know the stars." Her high-pitched cackle sent a shiver up Avery's spine. Her voice seemed somehow familiar, almost like a childhood dream he had never forgotten.

The four of them trooped out onto the tarred, flat space between a series of chimneys that gave a sense of protection against sliding down the tiled mansard roofs that were far too steep to save one's fall. Betty stood in the gathering gloom beside a brass-fitted telescope that all but dwarfed her as it pointed heavenward.

"Welcome to my little platform, gentlemen, and welcome back, you two." She nodded toward the ladies and turned back to her work without even acknowledging the others with a glance. "You are just in time to see me witness what I fear may be a cataclysmic finding, one that no one has seen for a least a millennium and possibly longer." Her back was bent in an unnatural curve as she sighted through the scope at an object the others could only fear to imagine.

Avery desperately wanted to ask what the subject of her search might be, but found himself unable to speak. Damien glanced from his new friend to the hunched form of Willy's mother, also unable to utter a word. Sounds of what seemed like incantation came from their hostess as she concentrated on her work. Singsong, high-pitched, almost-wailing strains of an apparently ancient language softly rent the air. Avery was sure he could see the airwaves vibrate.

Even Willy was struck dumb by the scene. The five of them huddled by the door waiting, all but mesmerized. At last came a cackle of delight as the last light of day faded and Betty's search ended.

"There we are, my lovelies. Discovery! Eureka! The Great Dismal Swamp of a billion years ago!" She did a little jig, all but undetected beneath her long skirt, and turned to declare her finding. Looking directly at Avery now, she pointed a bony finger in an accusatory fashion and burst out laughing. Everyone flinched, even Willy.

"This is what you were looking for, I believe, Master Astronomer. Proof of the dark powers that pervade the universe. Yes?" Her voice rose into a subdued shriek. "Only those of us who have practiced the unmentionable can even hope to know what the implications are. Only those who feel the forces of Nature pulsating within our veins can ever hope to know the full meaning of Creation." Her eyes went wild, and she suddenly shut up, seeing the reaction by all to her pronouncements.

"It is what a great number of us are curious about, Mistress Betty, as proof of something beyond our ken looms ever closer to the surface of our comprehension." He immediately regretted taking on the professorial tone as he saw the wicked twinkle in Betty's eyes.

"'Something beyond your ken' indeed, Master Astronomer—so far beyond your understanding that you might as well wear a dunce cap and kneel before the altar of ignorance in your shorts." She stood frozen now, looking for all the world like a satanic statue but for her flickering eyes that went from one to the next of her guests with a burning look of interrogation. "When was the last time you encountered the stench of birth, Master Astronomer? The cries of the dead or the wails of the forgotten?"

Willy was sobering up quickly now. "Mother, you really should show some—"

"Quiet, you child of despair, you mote in the eye of reason."

Willy made an effort to lurch toward his mother, as Fiona and Missy each grasped an arm to hold him back. "If I be such a mote, then it is you who made me so, Mother. You..." His voice choked into silence.

Damien was the first to try to smooth over the scene. "Is it possible, Mistress Betty, that you might explain to us all the meaning of your 'Great Dismal Swamp'?"

Betty eyed the young man with sudden interest. "Now, why didn't I think to do that very thing?" She nodded and adopted an air of restrained ease. "The Swamp' is a vast wasteland of pulsating gases that devour all celestial matter that comes close." She raised an arthritic hand as a quick gesture to allay questions. "No, it is not a black hole, as many of you might suspect." Her eyes took on an almost tender look of faraway longing. "It is more like an ocean of opposites that attracts all in its path, all things of all descriptions, even unto time itself."

"But surely that is what we understand black holes to be." Avery knew there was something he couldn't quite put a finger on but hoped he might cajole a further explanation.

"Not by our calculations, Mister Smarty-pants. A black hole is the remnant of a collapsed star, as you know. It serves to draw into it, by dint of enormous gravity, everything in its vicinity, even light. But"—her hand shot up with unusual vigour—"black holes are merely Nature's punctuation marks. Her angry moments, if you please." She cackled quietly, as though to a nearby friend. "The Great Dismal Swamp, on the other hand, has a mind of its own. It lives and breathes. It hungers and hates and exists to destroy, to balance the forces around it that make desperate efforts to create." Her eyes opened wide—deep brown, like the cat's.

Everyone stood mesmerized by this statement. Damien looked from Betty to Avery and back. "Then this could verify what our friend here has postulated." He leaned forward eagerly. "If your swamp has a mind of its own...then it might just be the obverse of the known universe and—"

"Did I say that?" Betty feigned anger. "Did I say that it was the obverse, the other side of the coin, from what we can see?" She shook her head. "What fools ye mortals be. What blind and helpless fools. The Swamp is the cradle of all existence. It is the endless return to nothingness that is the hallmark of life. It is the end of the beginning and the beginning of the end."

"May Mr. Churchill not spin in his grave." Avery blinked and looked to study the enraptured expressions of the ladies.

CHAPTER FOUR

"Whatever do you make of what that old crone had to say?" Damien drank long and deep of a tankard of ale in Avery's usual watering hole, the Mole and Hedgehog.

Avery looked around to be sure of his bearings and to check that no one was inordinately interested in their conversation. "She seemed to confirm to me," he began tentatively, "the basic principles of dark matter as I understand it, with the helpful addition of an animistic interpretation that imbues spirit, if not reason, to the bloody stuff."

"Yes. Most interesting…and weird, don't you think?" Damien looked around conspiratorially all of a sudden, himself. The ladies had excused themselves summarily outside the pub, and now the two men were free to express their minds without concern for criticism or hurt feelings.

"What gets me," Avery all but growled, "was the fact that the old biddy acted as though this swamp factor has been known down through the ages—to the right people—that it was a basic truth any numbskull should know."

Damien nodded. "Any numbskull with the right training." He arched his eyebrows in disbelief.

"Yes, old man, where is your family heritage of curiosity in the ancient arts when we need it?"

"Well, I must admit to more than a tingle when she was going on about the role of the swamp factor, as you call it. I fairly levitated at the thought of such a sinister force up there."

Avery raised a finger with a subdued motion. "That is what puzzles me particularly, don't you see? What she was describing was more of a cinematic, fictive force that we can see in vampire movies any time, not what I would have thought to be the probable scientific reality that we presume is dark matter."

"You mean you think she could be taken in by Hollywood and the frenzied minds of screenwriters?" Damien frowned as he tried to think that through.

"I just don't know! That is what is so galling. You and I have what appears to be a very limited insight into any of this monkey business. Mistress Betty of Bournemouth has her own take on the whole matter, and science seems to be totally out in left field, hamstrung, unintelligible, blind as a…Ah ha! That may be it! What say you, Danny lad? Blind as a bat. Yes?"

"Whatever are you driving at, old man?"

Avery leaned forward and all but took Damien's jacket by the lapels. Letting his quivering hands fall to the table, he tried to compose himself. "Let's see if I can make sense of all this…Right." He swallowed hard and fixed Damien with a steely glance. "Bats, as we know, are not blind…hmm, hmm. But they use their exquisite sense of sound to find their prey, often tiny bugs such as mosquitoes that are no slouches when it comes to aerial acrobatics, themselves."

"Yes, yes. We all know that." Damien frowned more deeply as the direction of the conversation continued to elude him.

"Bats are known throughout history to be dwellers of not only dark places but of cavernous equivalents of Hell." Avery paused to try to make an invisible link take hold in his mind.

"Well, from my own experiences spelunking in the American Southwest, they make the caverns hell-like with all their guano, you know. Quite a stench, really. And often deep. 'Deep bleep,' as they say in the States." Damien feigned the look of a bohunk as best he could.

"Levity is not what we are after here, Danny lad." Avery frowned his disapproval. "Give me a moment. The idea is trying to slip away, trying to elude me…Damn!" He banged his tankard on the table, drawing the attention of several nearby souls and the waiter, who presumed he was reordering a round. "Now I've lost it. Bloody hell!"

"We do hope not," Damien replied under his breath.

"Oh, lamentations!" Avery looked up at the approaching waiter and was relieved to see that he was bringing another round. "Just what I need to drown my sorrows, dull my wits, and forever lose the gist of the thought that was so close to"—he raised both hands as though strangling an invisible victim—"letting me through some magical door that I never before knew existed."

"It will come back to you, old man." Damien grasped his new tankard with unnecessary force, feeling the frustration as well. "Something about hypersensitivity, I suspect, yes?"

Avery slumped in dejection. "I haven't the foggiest idea now," he admitted. "It just evaporated from my mind, as though on orders from above." He shot an accusatory glare at the ceiling. "So now we are back to square one or the sandbox or whatever bloody pit of Hell such frustration rises from."

"Now, now. We haven't sunk that low just yet, old man."

Avery cast a vacant look at his new friend. "And what makes you say that? What evidence have you that this table, this pub, this sacred isle has not been visited by...something we can neither see nor even define?"

Damien was caught up short. "Well," he paused, "what is to say that we are not in a constant state of being visited by...whatever it is?"

"Precisely, sadly, my point." Avery sighed, throwing up his hands. "If a fraction of what we can put together between the suppositions of science—an oxymoron of its own—and the assurances of an old crone like Mistress Betty...is true, then we need to get a large shovel in hand and start some mighty digging."

"Or some loud praying?" Damien took a self-consciously long draft of ale.

Avery gave him a frustrated, almost dejected look. "Do you remember the cinema *Star Wars*? And that wonderful idea that ran through it, about 'The Force'?"

"Oh yes. 'May the Force be with you.' Obi-Wan Kenobi and all that." Damien flashed a childlike expression of glee. "Of course, I remember."

"Well, don't laugh too hard at what I am about to tell you, then, as my nerves might not be able to stand the rejection." Avery raised a tired finger by way of warning. He tilted his head to one side and adopted a far-away look. "When I was growing up—long before *Star Wars*, of course—I remember my mother telling me that we were all the stuff of stardust. Something that Carl Sagan repeated to us all years later as a basic premise of his beliefs. And it is something that I have always made an effort to refute or prove, as the case might be." He paused to check for reactions.

"And lo and behold," he went on, satisfied that his listener was fully engaged, "the closer I got to a resolution of the problem, the more frequently I would run into Obi-Wan Kenobi. I mean literally." He shook his head in disbelief. "If only on a poster—they were everywhere in those days, of course. Or on the tele—an interview with Alec Guinness, who seemed quite content to go along with the message. Or in bookstores, on the underground, or even in Edinburgh, for God's sake—land of the stalwart individual."

"And superstitious lot," Damien was quick to add.

"Yes. And therein lies the rub." Avery's eyes lit up, if only momentarily. "We may have in the unlikely embodiment of the Scots the simultaneous existence of the bull in the celestial order of things and the...Just what is the sign opposite the bull, Damien?"

"Well, er, it's Scorpio, actually."

"The scorpion? Ugh, but how true to nature, what?" Avery did some quick computations in his head. "Hmm! If we know anything outside rigorous scientific findings, it is that opposites attract. Right?" Damien nodded, quite intrigued. "And we have to acknowledge that so-called opposites who marry or at least have children—say Europeans and Asians—more frequently than not have beautiful children...in the eyes of most any beholder."

Damien was catching the drift, but remained sceptical. "I say, aren't you putting the cart before the horse or—"

"Or my foot in my mouth, ever so inadvertently? Probably, but let me try and finish the line of reasoning that once again seems determined to elude me." Avery frowned, and his mouth curled into a silent curse. "Damn! I know I was onto something, and yet...once again my mind just goes blank, as though someone was shutting off a switch." He shook his head. "I suppose I am just getting too old to handle my liquor anymore." He shoved his tankard away with a growl.

A loud argument broke out toward the rear of the tavern. Two men stood and hurled curses at each other. Avery had seldom, if ever, seen anything like it, certainly not in the Mole and Hedgehog. One man now emptied his mug in the other's face. A scuffle ensued while the others at the table tried to separate the two. Chairs skittered across the floor, upended and looking for all the world like fallen soldiers to Avery.

"What the hell?" Avery stooped to pick up one of the chairs, almost feeling sorry for it. "Has all of London lost its head now that the Olympics are past and we are back to normal?"

"Fisticuffs and the Marquis of Queensbury are as about as British as tea in the afternoon, I believe—historically speaking, of course." Damien dodged a patron who rushed to join the fray. "But I do hear that the incidence is up for bouts like this—all over the country."

"The beginning of the end perhaps, eh, Watson?" Avery brought himself up short and sheepishly corrected himself. "I mean Damien, lad. Sorry about that, but the old Sherlock Holmes syndrome that so many of us suffer from slipped out quite uninvited."

"Quite so. As long as Dr. Moriarty doesn't show his evil self, we should be good to go."

"If only we were, dear chap. If only we were."

* * *

The pleasing sounds of fine stone under the tires of Rufus Aldrich's Minnie Minor as it rolled up the long driveway to Haulding House proclaimed the opulence that was the hallmark of the two hundred acres of finely manicured grounds. Rufus was no stranger to the old property, having married into the family several years earlier. While never made to feel at home, he had wilfully ignored the cold shoulders and warmed to the friendly staff, particularly the upstairs maid, and quite enjoyed the discomfort he caused the rest. Of slight build and red hair, well into the stages of recession, he seldom rated a second look wherever he went. Even the butler was reluctant to greet him and take his coat. Nothing, of course, was ever a secret for long at Haulding House.

"Had a good drive, did we, sir?" The head butler's nose was appropriately raised on high.

"As fine as ten pounds worth of petrol could be enjoyed, I suppose. Crickey, Barney, even with my Minnie, internal combustion isn't what it used to be." Rufus brushed back his thinning locks and barged by the patient butler, who refused to show the displeasure he felt at not being called by his family name of Barnes.

"As you say, sir."

"Is my wife, the beauteous Charlotte, anywhere about, or has she gone to town already?" Rufus did not bother to look back at Barnes as he surveyed the opulent front hall with its sweeping stairway off to the left, which led the eye to the first floor above, well decorated in finely carved railings along the open hallway. An ancient—he was told—candelabra hung high above the marble floor. It was obvious to his well-travelled eye that it was of relatively recent, if fine, vintage Venetian glass. His in-laws were never above a bit of creative ancestry to boost their place in life, whether in their bloodlines or in those of the furnishings.

Of course, Rufus was quick to uncover subterfuge among others since he had taken refuge in it himself upon occasion. His particular branch of the Aldrich family could be traced back no more than three generations, to horse thieves who had barely had a chance to procreate before meeting the standard punishment for their crimes. And the Wentworths were of similarly vague lineage. Even the source of their wealth was suspicious and certainly never discussed. That certain British reserve in such matters came in fine handy for them.

"I believe that Mrs. Aldrich has come down with a bit of a cold, sir." Barnes's eyes remained straight ahead, but his alert mind caught the discomfort his message delivered.

"What? Not again!" Rufus now glared at Barnes as though he were the cause of the news he conveyed. "Why, that's three times in less than three weeks. Whatever has become of my poor, pathetic wife? Is she some sort of hypochondriac all of a sudden whenever I return from a bit of a jaunt up-country?"

"I'll get your things, sir." Barnes made no effort to answer or bow as he turned to see to the luggage.

"Thanks ever so, Barney. At least I can count on you to come through when the going gets tough." Rufus raised his bushy eyebrows at that odd statement, dripping with sarcasm as it was.

"Very good, sir." Barnes motioned for the only footman on duty at the moment to remove Rufus's luggage, shooting stick, and coat from the car while he proceeded to drive it around back, well out of sight.

Rufus trundled moodily upstairs, wondering what he might accuse his wife of now. "Oh, there you are!" He all but fell through the door of his wife's bedroom. "I thought you might have rambled into town by now, but Barney says you've tripped up again over that wilful cold you caught last month."

Charlotte lay on her bed beneath a down comforter that hid her tall, slender body that had so beguiled Rufus so long ago. She moaned briefly, whether because of her husband's appearance or just her physical discomfort, Rufus was uncertain. Her large blue eyes, watery and sad, stared at him in silent rebuke. "If I only knew the cause of this fiendish cold, I would certainly act to rid it from my home forever." She reached for a tissue and proceeded to rid herself of a large quantity of mucus instead.

"And throw it out with the trash, eh, dear Char?" Rufus approached the bed with feigned concern.

"Where it would belong!" Charlotte's face lit up with the thought of such good riddance.

"I do wish you would let me use one of Aunt Matilda's formulas on that wretched bug that seems determined to drill through to your inner sancta." Rufus loved to conjure up words that cast suspicion on his background and intensions.

"My inner what? You are such an unprincipled man! I suppose that's the reason that I married you. That and the fact that my parents can't stand you!" She managed a woeful smile as she reached for another tissue.

"You are such a dear when you're sick. I should make every effort to… keep you in bed at least for a fortnight each month." He shot her an evil grin. "That should work out to everyone's satisfaction, don't you think?"

"Except for Libby, who absolutely dotes on you." Charlotte nodded toward the next room, where they could both hear the maid quietly humming as she polished the silver. "She's worse than I am, I have to admit."

"I needn't remind you that a fortnight is merely half a month, now need I, wifey dear?"

"You wicked man! No, you need not." She shot a glance at the Adam ceiling, beautifully crafted in the unmistakable design. "I suppose it wouldn't hurt to try one of those compounds of your aunt's, would it?"

Rufus straightened up and almost teetered over backward in disbelief. "Why, no! It wouldn't hurt a bit...at least it's not supposed to." He grinned as his eyes betrayed great doubt. He spun around on one foot in glee. "This will be nigh on historic! If only I can remember the incantations." He quickly raised a hand. "Just joking. No incantations needed with most of Aunt Matilda's stuff. No sirree!" He waltzed out of the room, and the sound of a loud swat and Libby's quiet protest could be heard as Rufus went about looking for the ancient leather case in which his family's doctoral theses could be found.

Soon enough he was back in her room, and Charlotte looked on in quiet amusement as her husband actually appeared to be animated about something. It had been his aloof disinterest in just about everything that had fatally attracted her to him in the first place. And now, years later, he seemed to be becoming a new man, a different person entirely. At first she was intrigued, but quickly she began to feel the ennui other men had always created in her. At least there was the excitement of taking a potion that might turn her into a lizard or a frog or whatever. Anything but the boredom of her current life would be welcome, she thought.

As Rufus circled around the room and held a series of vials up to the light, as though inspecting their souls, Charlotte began to feel quite giddy. This was way better than the usual videotapes and margaritas he plied her with when he was in the mood for sex. Who knew what might happen? That was her greatest excitement in life, the pursuit of the unknown, purely for the exhilaration of the unexpected. She had tired of all the drugs Rufus had brought home with him, but this was different. This was going to the edge, maybe even over the edge. This was interesting. As Rufus continued his little ritual, she began to get both excited and aroused.

"I do hope that whatever happens to me, I will be able to have multiple orgasms in whatever form I might take." Charlotte threw off her bedclothes. Her long, slender legs somehow glowed in the low light coming from the open window.

Rufus abruptly stopped his turns and flourishes. He eyed her legs and the now-open blouse that barely covered the gloriously sculpted body that seemed strangely new to him. He bit his lip. "Perhaps we should put off the cure until after the treatment," he said with a smirk that showed the gap in his two front teeth.

"Ah hah! No, none of that. I want to be writhing with desire when this concoction takes hold, not limp from your usual shenanigans."

Grimacing from the slight, yet oddly excited at the thought that his wife was about to enter a new and different world of ecstasy, Rufus accepted the denial. There might always be a chance, he realized, for a little action while the potion was working its wicked will.

"I don't think that we should try a little of this and a little of that. Agreed?" Rufus didn't wait for a response. "I think we should just go for the gold, the high podium, the brain blaster. Right?"

"I am just so ready for my brain to get blasted from here to...wherever. I can't see straight." Charlotte leaned back seductively against her pillows, opening her nightdress. Rufus nearly fell over from unaccustomed glee as his mind raced forward to what he hoped would be a successful conquest of this new spirit revealing herself before him. "Pour it into me, Rufus, darling, so that I can get on with it, get off with it...whatever." Her eyes closed slowly, even though she hadn't touched the contents of the vial her husband held just above her lips.

Rufus could not remember ever being called "darling." Not even as a child. It stirred thoughts that somehow contradicted the lust that was being generated by just being with Charlotte in her new mood of surrender and anticipation. It did not, however, deter him from gently squeezing Charlotte's mouth to form an opening, into which he poured more of the potion than he had planned.

"Oops! Hope that isn't too much for you, dearie." With the satin sheet that would never be the same, he wiped the slight amount that escaped her lips. Her body convulsed ever so slightly, as though in a dream. A low moan sounded as she turned to one side and appeared to fall asleep. Rufus marvelled at how lithely she lay, more like a...snake than a human, he suddenly realized. Her legs actually appeared to bend, in conjunction with her body, to fold in upon themselves, to coil, to...slither. Jumping up from the bed, Rufus retreated in horror. Something deep inside his head clicked to life, something he instinctively knew was his reptilian brain, the most ancient resident in his skull, the very core of his being.

The sound that escaped him was neither human nor animal, nor anything he had ever heard in his wanderings in the Amazon rain forest, the home of more primeval life than anywhere else on the planet. It had a rasping sound, a plaintive wail that he had heard only once, and it had scared the hell out of him—the hissing snarl of a Komodo dragon. How could he have made such a sound? He hadn't even so much as smelled the potion he had just poured into his wife's waiting mouth. And if he was making such sounds, feeling so odd, what might she be going through?

He squinted his eyes in hopes that all the apparent illusion would go away. And yet Charlotte's body continued to…shimmer. Now he could see that she appeared to be growing scales across her bare midriff and down her thighs. He dared not move, much less touch her for fear of…what? That he might grow scales, too? That he might continue to inhabit the mind, if not the body, of a fucking Komodo dragon?

A loud gasp sounded at the door to the bedroom. Slowly turning, feeling stiff and very strange, Rufus saw the startled face of Libby, the maid from the next room. She stood transfixed, a hand to her throat, her Irish eyes all but falling from their sockets. What happened next scared the devil out of him. He felt his tongue whip across his mouth, back and forth, well beyond the confines of his lips. The disgust he felt was nothing compared to the fear he saw in the eyes of this girl. She had nearly fainted and was just able to fall away from the scene and out into the hallway. Staggering away, making sounds of muffled retching, she finally let out a scream that brought Rufus back from whatever hell he had fallen into.

Glancing down at his hands, he nearly fainted with relief that there were no signs of claws or scales or any other manifestation of the evil that had somehow nearly taken command of his mind and body. But, looking over at Charlotte's now-writhing figure, he knew there would be a lot of explaining to do, even if he got her safely back from wherever he had dispatched her. Gingerly he lowered one hand onto her scaly stomach and tried to find a way to communicate with this creature his aunt's potion had conjured up.

"Great Caesar's ghost!" Charlotte's father stood in the doorway and quickly turned green. His wife, Muriel, took one look and collapsed behind him, a moaning pile of clothes and flesh. "What in the name of Beelzebub have you done with our daughter, you fiend?"

Rufus turned with a sigh of abject relief to confront this tangible manifestation of the real world. "I wish I knew, sir. We were just experimenting—"

"With that confounded lot of drugs you're so fond of bringing into my home?" Mr. Wentworth's face now turned from green to purple. Rufus was mildly impressed but knew enough to keep quiet.

"No, sir, none of those new-fangled drugs you can find on any street corner. No, sir. Just something that has been…in the family for a…number of years, sir." Rufus felt a faint pang of pride as he said this.

"You will pay for this, you young scoundrel." Mr. Wentworth advanced cautiously to examine his daughter. "What have you done to her? Why is she so…green and…weird?" He recoiled as his daughter raised a hand toward him, a hand that had grown inelegantly long.

Rufus hurriedly scrambled to the case of potions, looking for an antidote. Feeling for the first time that he could remember as though he actually amounted to something, his pulse slowed, and he instinctively reached for the vial he felt sure was the one he needed. "Just give me a minute, Mr. Wentworth, and I believe all our wishes will come true."

"If that were the case, boy, you would be gone in a puff of smoke." Wentworth remained aghast at the sight of his daughter writhing on the bed as though not only in a trance but under the spell of evil incarnate.

"Right, sir. I stand corrected. Not *all* of our wishes would be granted. But at least we should…might…get your daughter back from wherever it is she has wandered."

"Wandered? Why you impudent idiot! She hasn't wandered anywhere. She has been transformed from a perfectly beautiful young thing into this…this scaly, reptilian avatar!"

Rufus looked up at this curious choice of words. "Avatar? Did you say…?" He nodded and frowned, lost in thought.

"Haven't you seen the movie, you blithering dimwit? The transformation of wounded souls, disabled individuals, into powerful alternative forms through some mumbo jumbo that your collection of vials apparently can let loose." Wentworth stooped to investigate the contents of the battered case. "Where is the eye of newt and wing of bat, I wonder?"

"Gone with the end of our first Queen Elizabeth's reign, I suspect, sir. I really think old Will was reaching for it when he wrote that stuff." Rufus briefly looked up from his attempts to feed the new vial's contents to his transformed wife. Her mouth had distended along with the rest of her body, but at least he saw no evidence that her tongue had split and was testing the air as a true viper's would. "Just a little of this, doll, and you will feel much better," he lied to her. It really seemed as though she was in some state of ecstasy that she was in no hurry to leave.

"You know, Aldrich, I always knew you were a total loss as a human being, but if you get my daughter back from wherever it is you sent her, I will personally give you…the west pasture and a million pounds to build your own home with." The poor man stared down at his daughter's contorted features and gasped. She was beginning to breathe with a sensuous regularity that, with each rise of her breast, began to shed the scales that had all but encrusted her body. What neither man could comprehend was that the scales didn't just shed; they dissolved into a misty cloud of vapour that gave off a powerful stench. Rufus stood up and retreated from the bed, as did his father-in-law. Holding kerchiefs over their noses, they looked on in growing fascination as Charlotte's body took on more and more of its former human dimensions. First, the legs appeared to straighten and smooth out; the abdomen swelled as the scales dissolved and pulsated with increasingly human undulation.

"By Jove, Son, your crazy aunt seems to have known a thing or two after all, eh?" Wentworth stooped to try to revive his still-swooning wife. "Get up, Muriel. Be witness to our latest claim to fame, my dear. The miraculous recovery from an evil spell of our only daughter." He held up his clasped hands in prayer. "'Rejoice, beloved, for the sins of your ancestors are hereby banished into the darkness of the abyss.'" He caught himself up short. "Now where the Hell did that come from?"

Rufus looked at him as though studying an unknown specimen under a microscope. "I do wonder. I had no idea that you were that sort of a… Christian." He sprang a broad grin. "Dad," he added swiftly, doing the previously unthinkable gesture of slapping him on the back.

The discomfort of the moment threw their attention back to the bed, where the miraculous undoing of the spell on Charlotte was proceeding apace. Moans of disapproval began to escape her as signs of recovery accelerated. Her features distended in what could be interpreted only as a fierce objection to what was happening. Both men took a step forward as Muriel shook herself awake, screamed, and collapsed again. Libby stuck her head through the door, quite mesmerized by the scene, and tripped over her mistress with a moan.

"Damn!" The word was repeated with increasing frequency and ferocity as Charlotte's eyes began to quiver and consciousness began to surge back through her body.

"A miracle, I tell you." Wentworth's eyes all but bugged out as he saw his daughter regain her wits.

Rufus looked sideways at him, uncertain whether the enthusiasm stemmed from the recovery or the notoriety the family might enjoy. He didn't really care. All he could think about was the uncanny effect, it seemed, of his aunt's concoctions. Beyond the west pasture and the million pounds so impulsively promised by his father-in-law, he was already thinking about the millions he might make from television appearances, book offers, and sponsorships. He didn't at first register that his wife was fighting mad as she recovered.

"Oh, loathsome toad!" These were her first words as she came to. It was as though she might well be addressing some horror in her spectral state, saying good riddance. When her eyes popped open and she looked around, however, there was no doubt as to the object of her ire. "How could you pull me back, you bastard?" She gave Rufus one of her dirtiest looks. She sat up and saw that her parents and Libby were all there, enthralled. "What have you done to me?" She looked for something to throw at them all, to hurt them.

"What can you be saying?" Her father took a tentative step forward, knowing the full extent of her wrath that might yet explode. "Your devoted husband has brought you back from some horrible place that had you fast becoming some sort of...reptile." His wife fainted once more, and Libby began to scream and choke again.

"Yes!" Charlotte raised her arms high over her head and stretched, much as a cat might. "A reptile's life was looking far more promising than anything I've ever experienced around this pile of bricks. And you, you loathsome toad, brought me back." She squinted at Rufus with a wrathful snarl. "I'll have to remember that next time I find myself approaching... well, never mind."

CHAPTER FIVE

Avery Lloyd Owens couldn't sleep. He had a night-light he found oddly comforting of late, in spite of the ample amount of illumination seeping through the blinds from the streetlights below. Long before meeting up with Betty from Bournemouth, he had sensed there was something afoot, something indefinable and potentially dread that was closing in on his world. And the night-light was supposed to keep whatever that was at bay. And so it did but only to a certain point. There was this growing sense of something lurking, something sinister, something that needed more deterrence than just a little light.

He thought of calling Damien but checked his watch and realized it was far too late for that. He just wanted to uncover whatever he could that had led him to sense that there was such great tumult in the heavens. His basic thesis was founded on the appearance in the cosmic equation of dark matter. And the role of that new substance—one that had apparently always been there—seemed more subversive and destructive than anyone might have imagined. But how? And why now? What was the catalyst? And what was the consequence?

The stillness of the air in his room began to feel suffocating. He cleared his throat and got up to open the blinds. As he approached the window, the light, gauzy curtain hanging at its sides fluttered in a sudden breeze and caught the moonlight in a sparkling shower of incandescence. There was a moment when he imagined a sheer wall of light fluttered before his eyes, a wall that absorbed, or at least obscured, everything near it. He cocked his head. It had to be an illusion. He'd never seen anything like that before. And yet at the same instant he was certain there was a message in the phenomenon. Something was trying to communicate to him what it thought was both important and should have been obvious.

White light, moonlight, a diaphanous wall, and some variation on a black hole. What the Hell was going on? He quickly crawled back into bed and broke into a sweat in spite of the cool evening temperature.

"Damien, I'm sorry to be calling so late, but this is a bit of a…mystery, if not emergency." Avery's voice gave away his sense of urgency. "I feel as though…damn, I wish we knew each other better, but my old colleagues have long since written me off as bonkers, and you are my only—at least best—hope."

"Fire away, dear fellow, if that is not too foolish an expression." Damien's voice sounded calm and even eager in spite of the hour.

"I knew I could count on you. Thank God for young and unsullied minds. Well, here's my problem." Avery hesitated out of sheer embarrassment. "I am sure that someone or something is trying to communicate with me. And if that doesn't try your patience, I don't know what might." He found himself breathing hard.

Damien's voice rose a decibel. "My dear fellow, if anything is going to pique my interest, it is just what you have said."

"Tell me, young lad, what does the colour white mean to you?" Avery's eyes turned to slits as he prepared for the response.

"The colour white? Good lord, any number of things, I suppose. Wedding gowns, purity, those cursed gloves we used to have to wear—and the ladies still do at times—Christmas, at least in the States…What were you thinking?"

"I'm not sure, but I believe that you are close on a couple of counts." Avery swallowed hard and tried to continue. "Your mention of wedding gowns, ladies' gloves, and purity all resonate with something I think might be crucial to this puzzle."

"What puzzle precisely?"

"This white apparition I just saw. I wish I could explain it better, but there is too much that is pure speculation, pure possible madness on my part. But I don't want to let the moment go without…dissecting things as best I can, with your help."

"I'm not sure I like the sound of your choice of the word *dissecting* there, old man, but whatever help I can be, I am most willing." Damien tried to remain calm as he sensed that Avery was close to losing it. "So what, then, is the significance of the colour white for you?"

"Don't you get it? White…is the colour of yin, the feminine, as opposed to the black of yang—in the Taoist tradition, of course."

"Well, yes, that's true, but who said anything about Taoism?" Damien's voice became subdued and scholarly.

"Well, no one. But you know about the Mayan calendar and December twenty-first, 2012, of course."

"Yes, certainly. Came and went without a single shot fired. Go on."

"Right. No significant fireworks of the mortal kind, but the date was intended, according to some of my better informed colleagues, to summon in the predominance of the yin over the yang after all these millennia. The triumph of the feminine over the masculine. Surely you have heard that as well."

"Yes, of course, though mostly from my disconsolate Scottish friends, who are more intent on independence now than ever, seeing as they have lost their turn at being superior subjects of the crown." Damien allowed himself a soft laugh.

"How do you think the rest of us feel? In Wales there is a…oh, never mind. All that is just… politics. What I am trying to get at is a cosmic factor that may help us unravel the mystery of how dark matter is altering our destinies, our very futures."

"Well, that would be a breakthrough, wouldn't it? But how may I help in all this?" Damien's voice began to betray a level of frustration.

"God only knows!" Avery shook his head and stared into the darkness, where there had been that shimmering wall of light. "It's gone…I suppose that I am quite mad…How could any sensate being appear by my window and flash a sign?" He groaned at the absurdity of it all.

"Why don't we see how things appear first thing in the morning, eh, old man? You know how darkness does tend to…Isn't that funny?" Damien fell silent. "I was going to say something trivial about the darkness before the light, you know? And then…well, I still think there is some truth to the old saw about daylight bringing fresh insight and all that."

Avery bowed his head. "Of course. Of course, you're right. Daylight will clear all sorts of things up, I'm sure." He knew to his core that that was not true, but what could he say? How could he explain the gnawing feeling that there had been something in the room trying to communicate with him? And he had failed to be worthy of its faith, its trust in him, that he could understand whatever message it had for him. "Thank you, Damien, for your patience, and at this late hour." He closed his phone and felt more vulnerable and useless than at any time in his life.

The first thing he did the next morning was to investigate the curtain that had shone so brightly. Nothing in its fabric or position or place in the room seemed to correlate with the optical experience he had witnessed. It didn't even smell odd. There was no brimstone, sulphur, or any other hint that there had been an alien presence, or at least message, connected with it. The thought that he might indeed be going mad brought sweat to his forehead and a ringing in his ears. He retreated to the tiny kitchen, where he had a store of vitamins, and sought out something for blood pressure.

Damien was at the door at precisely nine thirty. "Well? The sun is up, and the birds are all atwitter. How does that...experience stack up now?" His voice was unnaturally chipper.

Avery stepped aside and swallowed hard. "Not a damned bit of good, you know? Everything is still with me—everything but the answer to the puzzle, the proper response to the initiative, whatever the hell it was that I was expected to do."

Damien peered closely at his new friend. "So the analysis remains the same, does it? A definite message sent from some unknown source that you...buggered up?"

"Precisely! Buggered and blundered and failed completely!" Avery let out a deep breath of frustration. "Come have some coffee and take a look around. See if you can detect something that this old fart has missed in his onrushing senility."

"Now, now. Let's not be quite so hasty to put that foot in the grave. There are too many variables for me to even begin to judge who might be senile and who might be extraordinarily prescient."

Avery managed a weak smile of gratitude. "Perhaps you would rather have some tea. I can always put the kettle on. Won't be a moment."

Damien politely refused the offer and proceeded to the sight of the apparent miracle. "Seems perfectly normal, doesn't it? No burn marks, no rips. Quite tidy little place you have here." He looked around admiringly.

Avery just grunted and poured himself some more coffee. Then he perked up visibly. "*Tidy*. That's the very word that has been going through my head since last night! However did you…Of course, you didn't." He peered at Damien with growing frustration. "Now, how does *tidy* fit in with what I imagined happened last night?"

"I say, old man, *tidy* is the watchword of all women everywhere." Damien ran a finger over the windowsill. "Thank God there is some dust here, so you needn't take this personally. But it has been my experience that there are no limits to which a woman will not go to be sure she has a tidy home." He broke into a broad grin. "You know, I have always thought that if it were not for women, we men would be sitting around the front of the cave, sunning ourselves, belching at will, and swatting at stones with a crooked stick." He laughed out loud. "Enjoying life instead of chasing after the holy grail of financial security and social respectability."

"My dear fellow…how astute you are." Even Avery broke into a smile at that.

"But you see," continued Damien, "the word *tidy* denotes femininity, and that is what you felt was the defining presence here last night. Correct?"

Avery seemed quite lost at first, but then gathered his thoughts. "Yes, I see…perhaps." His shoulders slumped dejectedly. "But where does that lead us?"

"You were saying on the phone that there had been a definite feminine influence associated with whatever message was being sent. Remember?"

"Of course, yes. And that the Mayan calendar event ushered in the age of yin…yes." He paused, lost for words. "But that leaves me no closer to understanding what happened than before."

"Give it some time, old man. These things can take a while to sort themselves out." Damien slapped his friend on the back. "Particularly where a woman is involved."

"Not to mention all of Creation, which, by the way, I have always felt was the specific domain of the woman, the yin principle." Avery eyed his compatriot cautiously for his reaction to that declaration of faith.

"Quite" was Damien's instinctive response. "Mother Nature, the Creator of all things…decidedly feminine."

The two sat at the dining table just outside the kitchen and agonized over their plans to decipher the challenge they both knew could be a lot more important than either was willing to admit.

"I think we need to contact those two ladies and their apparent mentor, old Betty the hag," Damien concluded after all too short a while. "If there is a feminine entity at work here, as you suspect, the least we mere mortals should do is consult some of the practicing faith." He leaned forward in a gesture of capitulation.

"Spoken like a man's man, my boy. Do you think we can find that odd pub they liked so much? The What and What?"

"The Goat and Dragon, I believe it's called. One of those latter-day attempts to capture the whimsical nature of our prehistoric past." Damien shook his head. "Not so prehistoric or, I should say, not so past, come to think of it."

"Only one way to find out." Avery rose stiffly to his feet. "Let's away, then, Lancelot, to seek out dragons and hope to dodge the consequences."

Several frustrating misleads later, they finally arrived under the sign that marked their destination. Damien was the first to note the small insignia in the lower left corner of the crude depiction of the two namesakes. "Well, well, the mark of the pentacle. I might have known." He looked around for noticeable landmarks. "I strongly suspect that this establishment only opens at certain times, and by that I mean it only appears, at least to the likes of us, when it so chooses."

"I don't doubt that for an instant, old friend. Let's get ourselves inside before it decides we are unwelcome and dematerializes, or whatever it does." Avery placed a hand on Damien's shoulder as the two cautiously crossed the threshold into the pub.

An icy silence that surprised neither one greeted them.

A voice finally broke the silence from the dark interior. "Your lady friends are not here just now…if you would like to come back some other time." The voice was familiar, that of Betty from Bournemouth.

Avery took a bold step forward. "We were actually hoping to remake *your* acquaintance, Mistress Betty. The young ladies would be a fair bonus to our search, but it *was* you we were hoping to talk to."

A low hum of conversation broke out, and both men felt it safe to breathe again.

"If it's an argument you want, you can save your time and mine," Betty's still- disembodied voice muttered above the growing sound of low voices speaking in unison. Or chanting. Neither Avery nor Damien was quite sure which.

"We certainly are after no argument…only clarification of a point or two." Avery took another tentative step toward the dark interior of the room, followed closely by Damien.

"Clarification! Now, that is a very large word for a very small… thought." A knowing cackle stirred several heads. "Is it possible that a member of Britain's fine establishment has come to listen to an old crone speak of things beyond the imaginings of most?"

"It is that very hope, indeed intention, dear lady, that brings us here." Avery made a particular gesture to include Damien. "We would be most grateful for whatever you might wish to tell us about that Great Dismal Swamp you mentioned the other day and any other matters that might help us to understand the…current goings on in the firmament."

"Current? You fool, those 'goings on,' as you call them, have been there for all eternity. And"—her features now appeared as though floating on a cloud not far from the bar—"I am no lady."

"I stand corrected." Avery gave a slight bow. "We had hoped that you might…help us to understand the force that the Swamp holds over things…you know, its surrounding features, the cosmic bodies, whatever there might be…"

A loud sound of disgust ushered from where Betty's head had been as she apparently turned on her heel and prepared to disappear toward the rear. The crack of a stick being struck against the bar brought everyone's attention around, just as her full body now floated into view a few feet before the amazed duo. "'Whatever there might be,' you say?" She choked off a laugh. "'Whatever there might *not* be' is better put." Her beady eyes looked straight across at Avery as he stared at the empty space beneath her feet. "I only do this when mightily aroused—you might wish to know. When I must deal with the pathetic limits of mind that come our way, *if* they come at all." She was holding a large staff that appeared to be holding her off the ground quite effortlessly.

Avery and Damien stared in amazement, unmoving. Slowly she floated down to the floor and turned to spit into an old brass spittoon just behind her. The all-but-regal bearing she had exhibited while floating disintegrated as she touched down, her bent and crippled demeanour returning.

"What is it, then, that brings you here? Something has allowed you to find us." Her wrinkled features betrayed a look of keen wonder.

Avery and Damien exchanged knowing glances. "It is nothing more, or less, than a certainty that changes are in the making—cosmically—that no one of us understands, but you...do."

The old crone seemed to grow again, though her feet remained on the floor. "I *might* know a thing or two, yes." Her eyes appeared to give off a strange glow. She motioned to a nearby table, and the three sat. She positioned her arthritic hands toward the middle of the table, as though she were about to deal cards. The two men watched, almost in a trance, as her fingers moved like little snakes, individual cobras sinuously moving to a silent trumpet. Convinced that she had their attention, she continued. "The darkness that is the essence of the Great Dismal Swamp is all about us." She paused only briefly. "It allows some of us to come and go without being noticed on this plane. It allows our gathering places to appear and disappear, to be *and* not to be, all at once." She grinned as the two men caught the reference to Hamlet's soliloquy.

"It has been a marvel for all of us who...have witnessed your ignorance all these centuries. It is such a simple expansion of one's mind, after all, to understand the darkness." She shook her head with a piteous look at each of her audience. "All it takes is an open mind." She fell silent so that the two might either absorb her meaning or show their ignorance. Both shook their heads.

"Apparently this knowing," Avery began tentatively, "is based on experiences that are beyond us."

"No. Wrong!" Betty's face contorted once more. "Nothing is beyond you. It is simply a matter of blindness."

Both men looked more confused than ever. "But there has to be a formula, a special means of knowledge, that you all have"—Damien gestured around the room—"that we are not privy to."

A stifled cackle. "Hah. You are human, are you not?" Her eyes widened to show dilated pupils but not the cat's eyes that both men half-expected. "You have brains, have you not?" Her right hand thrust into the air angrily. "That is where you fail—you all fail—to see the universal truths. Your brains are no longer schooled to open up to the realities beyond the basics of reading, writing, and arithmetic." She turned and managed to hit the spittoon without effort.

"All it takes, gents, is an open mind. A mind that can hear the voices in the wind, that can listen to the trees and clouds and stars." She winced. "All peoples long ago could do these things. A few of us still can. All primitive peoples still with us on this planet know of what I speak. All of you with your advanced degrees in science—hah—history and business have encrusted your minds against the knowledge of the broader universe that is the true world we have inherited."

Avery felt a strange pang of pleasure at this denunciation. He had increasingly known that as he delved more deeply into his chosen field of astrophysics and astronomy, there was a curtain being inextricably tugged across his mind, a curtain that deprived him of a knowledge of the wider world. He had once marvelled at the definition of sophistication as 'the removal from the natural.' But now he understood. He frowned over at Damien, feeling defeated.

The younger man suddenly brightened. "You mean that the Bushmen of the Kalahari Desert in southern Africa that I used to read about—they understand the world that you describe?"

"They are among the few that remain, yes." Betty's eyebrows rose with serious satisfaction. "But their numbers are almost all gone, with the intrusion of the outside world."

Damien turned excitedly to Avery. "You remember those marvellous stories we all read about the Bushmen, old man? You must have read them, too."

"Some of my favourites. Yes, of course." Avery's features suddenly softened into a faraway look of sheer delight. "Who would have thought that those delightful people, those children of the stars, as they were known, might know the secrets of this age that we now all seek."

Betty just sat and watched the transformation that was happening before her eyes. A wry smile even crossed her face momentarily. "So, it was the spirit of the little people that brought you back here." She nodded, satisfied. "Very well, we can talk."

CHAPTER SIX

The two young ladies, Fiona and Missy, materialized mysteriously as Betty was laying the foundations of an explanation of her world to Avery and Damien. The latter two barely took notice beyond rising and offering a chair to each. The simplicity and profundity of what they were hearing mesmerized them. While Betty made no direct reference to dark matter or dark energy, the essence of her explanation was increasingly clear in terms that both men could understand. Particularly Avery, whose head kept bobbing up and down like a doll's.

The distance between Betty's world and his was excruciatingly slight once the veil of magic was lifted. The defining feature was the open mind she repeatedly referred to. A mind that can know of unseen forces can draw on those forces at will or at least with training. A mind that can incorporate an understanding of complex molecular structures at the same time as simple cosmic harmonies can venture far beyond the known universe, even into the darkest places.

"This is one of your world's greatest mistakes," Betty murmured. "You allow your minds to concentrate on narrow interests and foolishly sacrifice the ability to grasp the whole. For example," she said, gesturing to Avery, "when a star dies, all you can imagine is that the dust and destruction must create havoc. Explosions and death mean dust and destruction to you."

Avery bit his lip and said nothing. "While a few of you do seem to know that explosions and destruction can mean renewed life, the beginnings of a new cycle, it is not part of your philosophy, your religion, to admit that there can be more than one Resurrection." She squinted to try to conceal her chagrin.

"So religion has served to obscure reality, the true nature of our—your—world?" Damien sat back and looked at the warm glow of admiration on each of the ladies' faces.

"Some religions only," Betty was quick to point out. "You, young man, are among the few here who remain innocent enough to know this. There is no such limitation of thought in much of the rest of the world—Asia, the primitive peoples, many parts of Africa."

Avery didn't wish to discuss the difference between primitive peoples and much of Africa, so he pulled at his beard reflectively. He was still uncertain about the link between Betty's world and that of dark matter, but he was increasingly certain that one did exist and that it hovered near discovery. "Do you remember, Damien, when one of the American spacecraft was flying high over Australia and sparks were seen all around the craft? And that the Aboriginal people said that they had lit the fire to light the way for the Americans?"

Fiona and Missy squirmed excitedly in their chairs as Damien pointed at Avery, his mouth wide open, speechless. Betty watched the proceedings with quiet satisfaction.

"No one could ever come up with a reasonable explanation for how the sparks had risen several hundred miles through space to greet the ship," Avery continued, half in a trance. "Can you tell us how it was done, Mistress Betty?" He paused. "No, let me. I think I'm getting an idea how things work now." His eyes narrowed as he looked around at the expectant faces.

"The fire lit by the Aborigines was carried by the force of thought, or will, and could travel wherever it was directed through the good offices of...dark matter, the invisible element that exists wherever it is known to exist...by those who have the imagination, or wisdom, to know it exists." He let out a great sigh of relief as the ladies' response told him how clever he was.

"Well done, for a member of the Royal Society." Fiona could not suppress a smile. Missy clapped her hands and turned to note the general look of approval on Betty's face. A waiter appeared, as though by magic, and drinks were ordered all round, with Betty having a double whiskey.

"So," reasoned Damien hours later, "the mind controls the use of dark matter when properly understood?"

"I wish I knew. I seriously doubt that it's that simple." Avery closed one eye, as if to sight a target. "I suspect that while dark matter seems to play a pivotal role in what we call magic, there could easily be a reciprocal role for it."

"You mean that it dictates what can be transported or hidden or somehow manipulated?"

Avery raised a tired hand. "I just don't know, but there is definitely hope for some insight coming through after all we heard at the pub just now. What really bothers me is that there is no way to monitor this force—no way that we understand, at least—and therefore no way to influence its use."

"Or know of its intentions, if it has any." Damien scratched his neck dejectedly.

"Right, though the last thing we want to do is anthropomorphize this thing into some omniscient being, what?"

"Shades of Joseph Smith, I'd say, creating a religion out of…whole cloth." Damien rubbed his hands together, trying to concentrate.

"Or any number of would-be spokesmen for the Creator." Avery frowned at this thought. His shoulders suffered a spasm that caused his beer to spill skyward out of his mug. He glared at Damien. "That was close."

"What was close, old man?"

"The…nothing." Avery looked around to see if there were people looking his way. He felt particularly vulnerable. "It just occurred to me that this whole business is becoming less of a witch hunt, if you'll pardon the pun, and more of a story of creation somehow…" His voice trailed off.

"I keep going back to what Betty said about that myself." Damien raised an open hand and tried to explain. "She kept repeating that an open mind would see that death is life…that destruction is creation…that thought is deed. Or am I reading too much into it all?"

"Well, I don't know about 'the thought is deed' part, but the rest was quite clear to her. What we need to find out is whether we can decipher any of the dark side of her world and fit it somehow into the plan that I just know is about to tear this world apart." Avery clenched a fist. "I can just feel it. And sitting there with Betty made me all but resonate with…dread."

* * *

Rufus Aldrich had his own growing sense of dread. Ever since he had revived his wife from her reptilian reveries, she had taken a peculiar liking to him that he didn't appreciate. What was most unsettling was her tendency to wrap herself around him, as though she were still in her altered state. And the entire idea of a woman actually attracted to him for honest reasons was beyond him. The thought of ill-gotten gains, fame, and riches managed to keep him from showing his true colours. And he reasoned that Charlotte might actually just be after his future wealth. Her interest in designing their own home on the east forty was childishly giddy and did serve to keep her preoccupied for much of the time.

"Have you seen the latest drawings, lovey?" Charlotte swept into Rufus's bedroom without so much as a by-your-leave. Libby had left only moments before, and he hadn't yet had time to clean up. "Oh! Caught my little boy with his pants down, have we?" She pranced by him to lay down the drawings on the rumpled bed. "You really should have Libby make your bed up, you know, or the next thing we'll have a rebellion on our hands." She fixed Rufus with a withering stare. "She'll want to have me delivering you two your breakfast in bed, if we don't watch out."

"Heaven forefend!" was all Rufus could manage in immediate response. "Has that damned architect been whacking out yet more plans for our little cottage in the meadow, darling?" He pulled up his trousers and approached the bed. "You really need to rein that fellow in, you know, or he will have burned up the entire million just on drawings, and we'll have to settle for a brick outhouse as home."

"At least it will be brick, darling. And I believe the expression is a 'brick shit house,' isn't it? No need for undue propriety around this country girl, now, dear doofus." She shook her head, bewildered. "If only I knew why I have become so attached to you since you cast that spell…or rather, since you gave me that concoction of your Aunt Matilda's. There was a moment

51

there that you seemed to be quite different yourself, you may remember, just as I was going under."

Rufus had wanted to forget. He jerked around to confront his wife. "You mean you sensed something...about me as you..."

"Absolutely! You were becoming something quite deliciously hideous, I thought. Then that fool maid screamed, and I went on into my new world, which I have yet to recover fully from, I am happy to say."

"Are you ever going to tell me what happened, what you felt like?" Rufus was far more curious than he wished to let on.

"Someday perhaps." Charlotte shot him a look of sheer delight, knowing she was inflicting pain even as she drew pleasure from her memories.

Rufus was reduced to gazing at his hands and remembering his relief that they hadn't changed into the claws of a Komodo dragon. There was something so horribly inexplicable about being even remotely influenced by the potion that had him close to tears. "Obviously, you enjoyed your little sojourn on the other side a lot more than I was likely to."

"Don't be so sure, dearie. You just never got the chance to *become* whatever it was, so you never could experience life as that creature, you know?" Charlotte lowered her head and widened her eyes in a sensuously playful manner. "Who knows, even as a half man, half beast, you might really learn to enjoy life a great deal more...fully."

Rufus regretted his recent encounter with Libby that made his new desire to straddle his wife all but impossible. The mere allusion to beastly doings had him feeling uncommonly frisky. He briefly wondered how a Komodo dragon might go about tackling his wife but shook that thought off with a shudder.

"See what I mean?" Charlotte let out a smothered guffaw at her husband's obvious discomfort. "Who knew that there could be such pleasure among what we used to think were the lower strata of life forms? That songwriter—what's his name?—knew what he was talking about when he went into that song and dance about bees and birds and everything 'doing it.'" She twirled around, humming as her skirt flared out, revealing to Rufus her beautiful legs. She caught his look of uncommon discomfort. "Some other time maybe, huh, lover boy."

* * *

William Drury Hamilton growled at his mother's cat as it snarled, bared its claws, and dove under the couch. "One of these days, Euripides, I'm going to drop-kick you out that window, and I hope you land under the number ten bus and go 'squish.'" Somehow, such threats never made him feel that much better. There was always an air of superiority about the damned animal that gave him the willies.

"You ever touch that cat, and I'll have *you* drop-kicked out the window, and I'll be sure there is a number ten bus just waiting to run you over." Betty appeared out of nowhere. Willy shook his head, embarrassed yet again to be caught threatening his mother's favourite pet.

"Don't you ever knock? Can't a fellow get a few words in edgewise without being overheard by the goon squad of all sorcery?" He grimaced and sat down as heavily as he could on the couch, where Euripides was hiding.

"'Goon squad' am I now?" Betty raised a hand as though ready to throw a thunderbolt. She moaned as she barely restrained herself. "Of all challenges in life, why should you be my greatest?"

"Maybe as a reminder that you are not without fault, dear Mother." Willy quite liked that quick retort. He grinned a bit too broadly.

His mother again raised her hand threateningly, then spun on her heel to disappear into the kitchen. The ensuing cacophony of pots and pans being battered about was the sound, Willy knew, of his mother's frustration, not of dinner in the making. In the next moment, she was back to berate her son. "You know, you spawn of a shrivelled soul, you will tempt me once too often to do a foolish thing and…" She paused and bent over in pain. "There are energies aloft that I have not known before. I felt them strong with those two lads at the pub, the two that your friends dragged in."

"The astronomer and his friend?" Willy looked up and almost reached out to help his mother as she continued to be doubled up. "But they're just regular folk, barely human, I would say. How can they have influence over the forces that you call your friends?"

"If I knew, you simpleton, I'd…" Betty slowly straightened up and regained control over her anger. "If I knew, dear son, I would be most happy to let you know." She arched her eyebrows and let out a sigh. "I must remember to curb my bile. Always, if I lose control, I…lose control."

"And furniture flies and clouds carry venom." Willy looked subdued. "I know." He watched as the cat crawled out from under his feet and headed for the window. "What do you think you felt that those two have an influence over?"

Betty glanced at her son, wincing with pain. "I wish I knew. It would seem as though they have stirred up spirits that have been long subdued. But I have no reading on any of them. The only other thing that might be happening is…" She stopped, drawing in her breath hard.

"What? For the love of hellfire, what, Mother?"

Betty sat down slowly next to her son. Her face went ashen, devoid of emotion. "Only one thing I can think of, Son, and that is that the force of Darkness is emerging once more on this plane."

"Willy froze. "The force of…Darkness? I thought that was all over a thousand years ago."

"So did I, boy, so did I." Betty scratched at her wizened face. Colour didn't return. Nor did the slightest sign of emotion. "Only this time, there is something different…something far more sinister and destructive, I feel."

"Something more sinister than the Great Terror?" Willy grasped his mother's hand. "I don't think I like that idea too much." At that very moment, the window shook in its loose frame, the cat scrambled for cover once more, and the very walls began to shudder.

Willy and his mother sat embracing each other in sheer desperation as a deep rumbling growl grew ever louder and the building itself began to sway. "Holy shit, Mother. What the hell is going on?" Willy put his hands over his ears, thinking he could shut out the experience.

"Earthquake!" was all his mother could manage as she tried to get her bearings in the room that now threatened to fall apart. Cracks seared their way through the walls. Plaster fell from the ceiling. Dishes crashed onto the floor in the kitchen, as did all her precious belongings on the shelves around where they sat. She let out a shriek that faded into a wail. "Holy Beelzebub, this cannot be happening, not here in London." She stared at her son with a look of fear he had never seen before. "There is no reason…" She tried to stand, but a sudden lurch of the room sent her tumbling painfully into Willy.

Utter silence and stillness gripped them both, just as they tried to accept the chaos of the event. They stared at each other, uncertain as to whether they had lost their minds or their consciousnesses. Clouds of dust were the only moving witness to what had just happened. The stillness was even more unsettling than the chaotic noise it replaced. It seemed too unnatural, too laden with threat, too ready to explode into new destruction. There was a viscosity to the air that all but suffocated the two on the couch. The cat emerged, looking for all the world like a drugged rat.

Willy rolled off the couch and tried to stand. His mind was still buffeted by the crushing sounds and movement of the quake, and he fell back down with a cry of despair. His mother ignored him as she tried to assess the implications of the damage. It was not just her favourite pieces of porcelain that were shattered. It was far more destructive an event than that. But she dared not even think of the possible threat to her world, one that stood far more chance of destruction than that of her son or any mere mortals. Something there was, she now knew, that wanted control, that demanded domination of even her powers.

CHAPTER SEVEN

Scotland Yard's Inspector Graham frowned deeply over the report. "A bomb, you say? Without detonation? You mean the thing went off but didn't?" He dropped the report on his desk with a dismissive smirk. His tall, frail frame leaned forward to look once more at the implausible wording. "'The building is rendered uninhabitable, with fractures to the weight-bearing walls that would appear to be irreparable.'" His intense grey eyes looked up at the sergeant-at-arms, who stood like the proverbial deer in the headlights, shrugging and waving his short arms in dismay.

"That will be all, Sergeant. Get me Leftenant Forsythe, would you? Perhaps she can throw some light on what happened." Moments later the slightly overweight form of Lt. Forsythe sidled through the door, alert and all but impatient. "Ah, there you are, Forsythe. I take it that you have more than read this report?"

"Yes, sir. Much of it is my own work." She stood at ease, with the air of having gone through these interrogations all too often. A slight hand brushed back a loose strand of auburn hair. "Most peculiar, sir, I must say."

"You went through the building, did you?" Graham's gaze sought out any signs of stress or peculiarity on Forsythe's attractive features.

"No, sir. That might have been suicidal. By the time I reached the scene, the inhabitants had been evacuated—I really don't know how some of them got out—and the building was ready to collapse." Her green eyes widened at the memory.

"No smell of *plastique* or powder or any known explosive that might have caused the damage?"

"The only odour I could detect, and that was from near the entrance— as close as I could get, was that of sulphur, sir. Very strange. Very…eerie." She stood at attention unconsciously.

Graham looked from his trusted aide to the report and back again. He slowly grimaced and shook his head. "Sulphur, you say. Well, that is an essential compound of most old-fashioned explosives, at any rate." He painfully straightened his shoulders and asked a question he would rather never resort to. "Foul play by undetermined means, eh?"

"And undetermined motive, sir. The inhabitants of the building are an odd group of bohemian artist types and down-and-outers. No obvious rascals in the pigpen, as you like to say, sir." A slight smile stirred her thin, playful lips.

"And that leaves the owner of the building, wanting to cash in on his insurance policy. Look into that, would you, Leftenant?" Graham sighed deeply with the resignation of a veteran who has seen it all too often before.

"Very good, sir." Forsythe threw a sharp salute and retreated from the office, shaking her head.

* * *

Fiona and Missy had arrived on the scene minutes after the first emergency vehicles. Betty and Willy were nowhere in sight. A few dazed residents had made their way to the sidewalk, dragging what belongings they could gather before the building was liable to collapse. Bright lights flashed and flickered. A fire truck rolled out a conspiracy of hoses that squirmed on the ground with useless pressure, since fire refused to show itself. Confusion reigned and chaos strutted.

"Is there anyone still in there?" Fiona grabbed a passing fireman and gave her best impression of a damsel in distress.

"We surely hope not, ma'am, but there's talk of a cat and its owner, so we have men looking to do their best." The fireman touched the brim of his helmet and was gone.

Missy and Fiona grabbed each other's arms and simultaneously uttered the cat's name. With an unearthly screech, Euripides appeared in its third-floor window and leaped out toward the two women. Impulsively, each turned her back and leaned down. The cat landed with a loud sound of distress squarely on Missy's back. Letting out a sharp cry of pain, Missy felt the cat's claws dig deep before retracting to allow Euripides to land softly on the ground. Cursing loudly, Missy gave a half-hearted wave to the cheering crowd, who had witnessed the cat's safe escape.

"Well done, young lady." The fireman reappeared with a grateful grin. "That will save our lads a lot of trouble."

"But Betty, the cat's owner, may still be in there." Fiona took up the cudgel for the human side just as the building began to emit loud sounds of imminent collapse.

"Too late now, Miss. She's about to go, and I have to get my men out." Another brief tap to the helmet, and off the man went, shouting obscenities. As a great cloud of dust gushed from the front entrance, Willy appeared, dazed and blinded. Two escaping firemen grabbed his arms as they rushed to daylight. Fiona and Missy looked on in horror as the building just collapsed like a shot animal. Again there was an eerie silence in the immediate aftermath. All onlookers gasped at the total demolition as great swirls of dust plumed into the air.

Then shouts of disbelief rose first from the firemen and then the large crowd that had gathered. From the middle of the rubble, holding her precious staff as though it were from a royal court of the underworld, emerged Betty, white with dust but alive and looking quite in charge.

"Well, blow me down," Fiona managed feebly. "How is she going to explain this?" She turned to Missy, who was still nursing her back. "How do we manage to hush this up? It's going to be in all the papers any minute now."

Missy stopped squirming for a moment and looked around. "Do you see any photographers?" She paused to look more closely. "Do you even see anyone with their iPhones pointed her way?"

Fiona scanned the crowds now, too. "Holy Hades, she's done it again. Not an idiot in sight with a camera." The fireman approached once more. Fiona hazarded a statement. "It's a miracle. Look, that little old lady seems unhurt in all that rubble."

The fireman took off his helmet and brushed his hair back out of his eyes. "You won't believe this, I know, but we see this happen all the time." He shook his head and grinned. "Some people just aren't ready to go, you know, and there seems to be some…force that protects them…keeps whole buildings from falling on them. We see it all the time." He turned his gaze back on Betty with a look of unabashed awe. "You wouldn't believe what we see from day to day, and the papers won't even listen to us anymore. We just don't bother, you know, 'cause it's something bigger than any of us, beyond our knowing, even when we see it so often." He prepared to get his men and equipment gathered up. "You know that old girl, do you? Take good care of her. She is one in a million…or at least a thousand." He shook his head in disbelief and was gone.

Betty stumbled across the ruins of her home to where Willy had joined the two women. Admirers beat at the dust on Willy's jacket and looked on slack jawed as Betty approached. Fiona and Missy tried to conceal their trepidation with relief.

"Did I see Euripides get out OK?" Betty paid no attention to the on-lookers, who wanted to touch her and equally ignored her son. She gave a sly look to Fiona and a reassuring wink. "Takes more than an old pile of stone to slow me down, huh, sister?"

"We are so relieved, Betty. You have no idea. The nice fireman who spoke to us says he and his men see this happen all the time." She shrugged.

"All the time, is it?" Betty frowned. "Why they don't have the first fog-gy clue as to what just happened…but"—she smiled through all the dust that encrusted her head to foot—"that does make matters simpler, doesn't it, Son?" She wacked Willy on the back and shook her head. "I guess we get to go to the nearest shelter now and take up the life of true gypsies."

"No such thing!" Missy put a tentative arm around Willy. "You're both going to come and stay with us, for as long as you like."

Betty stood taller than her son had seen in a long time. "That would be asking too much, dearie. Especially now…considering what just hap-pened." She looked back at the pile of rubble. "Times, they are a changing, and I'm not too certain that they aren't going to get a whole lot worse before long."

None of the residents was allowed to sift through the remnants of their homes. The police cordoned everything off and explained that there had to have been explosives used to cause such complete destruction. Forensics had been called in. Reports would be made, and then retrieval of whatever belongings were salvageable could follow. All very routine, they were assured.

"At least they don't have their heads stuffed, the way the Yanks did after 9/11," someone ventured.

Betty suffered a violent tic when she heard that. "Damn, that reminds me. The evil perpetrated that day was as foul as most anything in the so-called civilized world since the Crusades." She squinted at Fiona even as she held on to Missy's arm as they left the scene. "Nothing has been done to contain that evil. No effort has been made to blot out the dark energy let loose that day. No one has even been held accountable." She cast a tired eye up at Willy. "What would you do, Son, if you had lost someone that day?"

Willy didn't pause but a moment. "Well, Mother, I am generally opposed to vivisection these days, but I think the ones responsible for that day should be drawn and quartered, the way they did to my great-great-ancestor, William Wallace."

Betty nodded her approval and let out a cackle that was choked off by the dust that still clung to her clothes and hair. "Very good, Son. America needs a bit of primeval justice doled out for that act, just to be reminded that they are part of this wider world we all inhabit."

"But, Betty, you aren't saying that 9/11 in New York was related to what just happened to your home." Fiona leaned close to hear the response.

"All evil is related, child, but I am not one to know how much energy they share. All I know is that what your scientist friend calls 'dark matter' is sensitive to the presence of evil and gains strength from it, as vampires thrive on blood."

"Now, Mother, there is no such thing as vampires, and you know it." Willy stumbled on a root and fell into his mother.

"You clumsy oaf. Of course, there's no such thing as vampires. I was just seeing if you were paying attention." She swept some of the dust from the front of her skirt. "But the likeness exists. Evil grows from evil and infests the dark places that we use to conceal ourselves and our intentions, when we so choose."

They all stopped in their tracks. Missy spoke first. "You mean that the powers we have are derived from terrible acts of destruction? That we are the pawns, then, of this dark force?"

Betty shook her head and spat. "There is nothin' I know that confirms that, I'm greatly relieved to say. But there is no doubt in this grey head that the force we draw on for our...work coexists with what others can draw on for evil ends." Her eyes went from one face to the next. Each was contorted by doubt and pain. "That is not to say that we are in any way like the assassins and terrorists and merchants of death and deception. But... we draw from the same fountain, we bathe in the same pool, and we need always be alert to trickery."

Willy put his arm around his mother. "Why, Ma, that's the closest thing to poetry and politics I've ever heard you say."

Betty dug an elbow into her son's side. "Don't you go and get affectionate with me at this late stage, boy." She looked up with mixed emotions. "That wouldn't be fair, now would it?"

Willy looked both puzzled and hurt. "I guess not, no." He raised an accusatory finger at his mother. "But you are always telling me that life ain't fair, now aren't you?" He chuckled in spite of himself. "So brace yourself, Mother. There might be hope for us yet."

Fiona gave him a hug. "Way to go Willy. Way to grow."

Everyone's spirits lifted even as dusk gave way to darkness and streetlights came on all around them. If relief couldn't be found as company for this little band as they made their way through London's North End, at least there was a palpable sense of purpose being born.

CHAPTER EIGHT

"Well, Leftenant, this report of yours leaves us high and dry, does it not?" Inspector Graham thumped the wad of papers with a tired fist.

"Sorry, sir. But there seems to be no probable cause for the owner of that building to have wanted it down. The records show that the rent he was receiving kept him in good stead. How, they didn't stipulate, but he hadn't paid his insurance for several years, so—"

"Bugger all! That leaves us, as I said, with nothing to go on. What are the forensic reports telling us?" The inspector reached for his meerschaum pipe and idly filled it with tobacco he knew he couldn't light.

"Nothing that I can make sense of, sir." Forsythe frowned as she took a tentative step forward, trying to articulate her confusion with body language. "It seems as though the damage was caused by a seismic event, even though our instruments picked up nothing." She waved her hands in the air. "The evidence points to a violent upheaval possibly caused by—this makes no sense, of course—the presence of sulphur."

Inspector Graham rolled his eyes. "Sulphur again. A major component of the realm of Hell, as I recall, Leftenant Forsythe. Perhaps what we are dealing with is a messenger from the nether regions. Could that be?" His voice dripped with sarcasm.

Forsythe swallowed hard. "Of course not, sir. At least, that is nowhere to be found in the report, sir."

"Most amusing, my good woman. Go on. I can sense one of your patented brilliant insights about to spring to life."

Forsythe clasped her hands in dismay. "The report does say that the building appears to have been shaken to pieces, which would corroborate the findings, or lack of them, on our seismic gear. It would also fit the findings that there were no explosives detected."

"Good God, woman. Are you trying to tell me that someone picked the bloody thing up and shook it to bits?" Graham sat down hard in his swivel chair, almost losing his balance.

Forsythe raised both hands in defeat. "That is what the report would have us believe, sir."

"What in God's name are those ninnies smoking these days, eh, Leftenant?"

"Whatever it is, sir, it must include a good dose of that sulphur, I suppose." She winced at the failed attempt at humour.

Inspector Graham ignored the comment as he turned to search his bookshelves for a long forgotten study he had written in college. "You know, Forsythe, this reminds me of a case I wrote about lo these many years ago at Cambridge." He stuck his unlit pipe between his teeth and reached high up for a plain folder that had been lying limp for years between several tomes on medieval law. Muttering to himself about sulphur and what sounded like damnation, he plopped the study on his desk. "That will be all for now, Leftenant. I need a little refresher on a case that came up some…years ago. I'll call you if I need you." He never looked up from the folder that now consumed his interest.

Forsythe nodded and took a swift glance at the title of the study as she turned to leave. "Spontaneous Combustion and the Power of the Mind" had been scrawled in longhand with an earnest excitement.

✳ ✳ ✳

Rufus Aldrich was having another bad day. Libby had been fired the day before, having been caught by Mrs. Wentworth with her husband. And Charlotte was behaving strangely again, much as she had ever since his experiment with the family formulas. One minute she would appear sexually aroused, the next as cold as a...reptile. He had tried the old routine of margaritas and videos. Utter failure. He bore her scorn one minute for his puerile attempts, only to be greeted by cleavage and an undulating tongue the next. He was losing sleep. He didn't even feel like taking his little drives up north, where gratification waited in the form of a wantonly willing coven.

"When are you going to let me have more of that wonderful elixir your aunt gave you, Roofie, dear?" Charlotte slid her tongue across the generous width of her lips in a very unreptilian fashion.

"And risk losing you to a scaly end—not to mention the million pounds your father promised me?"

"But what's a mere million pounds in comparison to the raptures I was beginning to have before you brought me back?" She idly laid a hand high on his thigh as they sat together on her bed.

He looked down hopefully and reached for her exposed knee. "You have never told me what was going on in that world you were joining, sweetie. Are you going to let me know now?" Rufus's eyes almost crossed as he leaned in to touch her glistening tongue with his own.

Quickly she jerked her head back. "Only if you let me have some more."

Rufus scowled. "What happens if I can't bring you back this time? What happens when you cross over, when you are transformed into that... thing you were becoming?"

"Then I'll be in heaven, and you will have to pick up the pieces. Simple, laddie boy." Charlotte rumpled his hair teasingly.

Rufus leaned back and frowned. "But...I'd miss you terribly, of course. However a million pounds *is* a million pounds, and things being as they are..."

"No elixir, no magic, if you catch my drift." She leaned toward him, folding her shoulders in to reveal her breasts that already seethed with passionate anticipation.

Rufus looked down, then up into her promising eyes and swallowed hard. "All right! You win! They win!" He choked on the stupid joke. Rising with difficulty to his feet, he adjusted his trousers and bounded to the door. Returning moments later with the treasured chest, he paused.

"Why haven't you used this yourself? If you are so anxious to get back to wherever you were, I would have thought—"

"I tried to, stupid." Charlotte caught herself. "I mean 'dear soul.' But they all look alike to me, and the last thing I wanted was to take the wrong stuff. I might have wound up looking like a donkey and feeling like a mule, if you know what I mean." She tried to smile sweetly.

Rufus wasn't about to admit that he himself was unsure as to which vial was which. Adopting a professional air, he lifted several specimens to the light and judged that the emptiest one had to be the passport to Charlotte's fantasy world. With a wan smile he sat next to his reclining wife. "You just relax now, and we'll start your journey as soon as you're ready."

"Ready? You think I'm not ready, you foolish man?" Charlotte's body began to undulate suggestively. "Give it to me now, Roofie, and you'll never be sorry."

Rufus sniffed at the vial as though it were a vintage bottle of wine. He wanted to know how it had begun to alter his consciousness so drastically the last time. It even occurred to him that Charlotte might have been right about enjoying the completed transformation into a Komodo dragon. What the Hell, he thought. There's nothing in nature that preys on Komodo dragons. They are the king of the hill, even if it is really more of a dung heap. Better the king of something than the knave that he was.

Hesitating to pour some in Charlotte's open mouth, he was tempted to try it himself. There was an overwhelming urge to fall into a spell that might allow him to fuse with the energy that he felt swirling in his hand. The impulse grew as he watched the closed eyes of his wife, her body rippling with desire and anticipation. His hand began to quiver, spilling the contents on her throat. He watched in morbid detachment as the precious liquid trickled down between her breasts. He looked at the vial and saw that it was almost empty.

With a shriek, Charlotte opened her eyes and reached down to catch what she could of the flow along her body. Sucking at her damp fingers and licking the palm of her hand with a savage intensity, she began to moan and writhe and curse profusely. Grabbing the nearly empty vial, she downed what was left and fell back on her pillows with a high-pitched wail. Her eyes swept back and forth across the room, looking for signs that the familiar furnishings were giving way to her other world. Frantically she reached up to grab Rufus's shirt collar, even as she looked down at her midriff that was bared and still unaltered.

"What have you done to me, you spineless piece of garbage?"

Rufus spluttered out an exasperated "Nothing, it seems." He was mesmerized by the sudden exhilaration at the failure of their tryst, their attempt to alter life. He had no clue as to why the formula had failed this time, except the faint realization that there had been a force at work this time that interfered with any previous results. For the first time, it occurred to him that the last event was mere hallucination, brought on by a combination of lust and chemicals. He had conned so many people using the same principles. Simple psychology. You get what you lust for. How Charlotte's father had been affected, he had no clue. Charlotte had desperately wanted out and she had been, after all, born in the Chinese year of the Snake, he remembered. How any of that jibed with reality was anyone's guess. Just then he began to realize that reality was anyone's guess. The master swindler and con man was getting a cosmic lesson of his own.

"Do something, you dreadful man!" Charlotte fairly quivered with distraction. "Are you going to leave me...to my family and your philandering ways?" She reached out to slap him and found herself stroking his chin instead. "It isn't possible that you actually care about me, I hope."

Confused as she was, Rufus shook his head vigorously. "Perish the thought, dear one." He tried to correct himself. "I mean, you dolt. The day I care for you would be the end of my freedom, my comfortable, carefree existence without a worry in the world."

"Then why are you holding my hand, you beast?"

"Good Lord, am I?" He looked down at his offending hand and couldn't move it. "It would seem as though I fetched up the wrong vial. I had no idea that Aunt Matilda had a love potion in that case of hers."

"A what?" Charlotte sat up and nearly bumped her head against her husband's. "You couldn't. You wouldn't."

"I just said that that would be the farthest thing from my mind, didn't I?" Rufus backed away briefly, then leaned in with something on his mind that he had never before experienced—affection. "Do you...?" He managed to choke off the rest of the question.

"Do I what?"

"I haven't the foggiest." Rufus shook his head like a dog ridding itself of water. He stared at the empty vial and gave it a sniff. "It would seem that we have been snookered by my dear Aunt Matilda into actually caring for each other." He raised his eyebrows as he reached for his wife. "I'm sure it will wear off shortly, but in the meantime...it does feel rather nice to...just be with you." He felt as puzzled as Charlotte looked.

"Oh, my God! That old witch!" She paused. "I do hope you're right, that it will wear off soon. The very thought of caring for someone gives me the hives. Don't you agree?"

"Absolutely." He stroked her arm. "At least I used to."

Charlotte gathered her nightgown around her protectively. "Now listen. This just isn't fair. All I wanted was to get sublimely lost in that other world you started to send me to, and the very same concoction has me... caring about you?" She made no effort to move. "What the hell is going on?"

"Beats the hell out of me." He lifted a hand and froze, tilting his head as though listening for some distant sound. "Did you hear that?"

"What, silly? No, I didn't hear a thing." Charlotte tilted her head as well and realized they looked like a pair of parakeets on a perch.

"It sounded like someone laughing—far away down a hole, maybe. Must have been one of the gardeners." He patted Charlotte's hand and stood to return the vial to its case. "Funny mistake I made, huh?"

"Quite riotous, I'm sure. I just want to know how long this little spell is going to last. Is that asking too much?"

"Saints preserve us, no." Rufus frowned as he heard the words fall from his lips. He shot a worried look at Charlotte but kept quiet.

"I certainly never heard you use those words before, lovey. What *is* going on?"

"It would seem as though Aunt Matilda's Catholic background is shining through this experiment we were—or are—engaged in. Who would have thought that some ancient formula or recipe, as she used to call them, would so bend our minds? It makes me believe that there had to be a nook somewhere in our heads that harboured gentle thoughts toward each other."

Charlotte pursed her lips and tried to remain calm. "What a ghastly thought! You mean that the formula uncovered deeply buried instincts that we have been merrily disregarding all these years?"

"It's either that or magic, and as the world's greatest cynic, I propose the simpler explanation." He reached down to draw Charlotte to her feet.

"We might as well not fight it...as long as it lasts, that is." He looked fondly into her eyes. "After all, we might be back to our former selves any minute now, loathing each shared experience."

"What an intriguing thought!" She wrapped her arms around her husband and drew him close. "I don't know that I like the idea."

"What idea?"

"The one about...reverting. I don't believe I have ever felt quite like this before, and it does feel rather...refreshing." She gave him a warm hug and blushed. "Do you think we could make an effort?"

"I suspect that whatever spell we are under is of our own making, you know. Which means we might just be able to have a say in our future... doings." Rufus felt a strange presence in the room and suspiciously looked around until he realized it was himself.

CHAPTER NINE

A very paced back and forth, mumbling to himself. He had rushed to the scene of Betty's destroyed home and found the constabulary unusually obtuse. No one would let him near the ruins, even when he explained there had been an extremely valuable telescope on the roof that might well have escaped destruction. His credentials meant nothing. What the hell did it matter that he was a lifelong member of the Royal Society of Astronomers if he couldn't cross an occasional police barricade? He telephoned Damien and asked to meet him at their pub. He needed a drink.

"Can you believe the basic caveman attitude those bobbies are showing?" Avery ordered a pint for each of them.

"Haven't you heard?" Damien nodded to the barkeep as his ale was slid expertly down the length of the bar. "There is a considerable kerfuffle at the Home Office over this whole matter. They think someone has come up with a new type of explosive that evades detection, and they are bound and determined to find out its composition, its formula." He drank deeply. "Scotland Yard is tearing its collective hair out over the whole mess, and the Yanks are keen to be let in on any investigation."

"Good Lord, you mean we're going to have a bunch of CIA chaps running around, sniffing at every brick and batten?" Avery ordered a whiskey chaser. "I must admit, though, that the entire business looks fair peculiar. Have you seen the pile of what's left?"

"Not yet, no. I understand that nothing else in the area was remotely damaged, which does lead me to believe that there was something"— Damien lowered his voice—"quite unique to the case, as they say on *Masterpiece Theater?*"

"And the upshot is that Betty was still in the building when it collapsed and walked out like the Queen of Sheba, covered only in dust." Avery reached for his shot of whiskey with glutinous gratitude.

"There is some talk that a similar device to the one that apparently helped to bring down the World Trade Towers might have been used— speaking of dust." Damien kept his voice low, leaning close to Avery's ear.

"Great Scott! I hope to God not." Avery paused to think of the consequences. "What am I saying? That would be a welcome alternative to what I think in fact did happen, monstrous as your idea is."

"Not my idea, please. Just one of many speculations that have stirred up a regular hornet's nest at the Home Office."

Avery frowned, wanting to break down and cry. He really needed more rest than he had been getting lately. "If I weren't sixty-two years old, you know I would just want to abandon ship." He shook his head with a tired resignation. "Really, the whole world seems to have gone straight to the dogs, and there isn't a single bloody thing I can do about it." He thrust a determined finger in the air. "Except this one last tilting at the Big Windmill." He laid a grateful hand on Damien's shoulder. "And if you will be my Sancho Panza, dear Damien, there just might be some hope for this weary world down the road."

"I hereby pledge you my fealty, my liege." Damien extended his hand, and for a brief moment Avery's spirits rose.

"What keeps me up at night now is the growing sense of despair that things are truly out of control, you know?" Avery tried in vain to resist downing his whiskey in one swallow. He kept his eyes on a bottle of brandy at the back of the bar but leaned closer to Damien. "There is just too much evidence that there are forces coming out of the woodwork that I have never sensed before, forces that seem ready to do the lot of us in."

"You mean like whatever it was that destroyed Betty's home?"

"For one, yes, precisely. But that appears to be only the tip of the confounded iceberg. Don't you see?" Avery managed not to order another whiskey. "It would seem as though there is a force that is playing with us, toying with the universe, almost, and enjoying every agonizing moment that makes me feel that we are all being loaded into a slingshot and are about to get hurled out into deep space."

"Good Lord." Damien looked at his friend and felt a sudden pang of sorrow. It wasn't just a fleeting personal reaction, he realized. There was something far more profound, more unsettling, than anything personal. It shook him to the core, but he knew he needed to conceal whatever it was he so viscerally felt. He was now, after all, the bearer of the burden of companionship on this seemingly ill-fated adventure. Sancho Panza 2.0. "Whatever can we do?"

"That, my dear Damien, is the $64,000 question." Avery turned to look directly at his friend. "Did I just stumble on a possible explanation for all of this?" He pushed back from the bar and stood with a vigour he hadn't felt for weeks.

"Whatever are you talking about? Wherever are you—are we—going?" Damien stood to follow the quickly retreating form of his friend.

"I haven't the foggiest, but I do know that if I start to accelerate my mind, to increase my metabolic rate, in effect I may just stumble on an answer."

"I see." Damien caught the barroom door as it hurtled toward his face while Avery exited ahead of him in what appeared to be the race of his life. Damien watched with increasing concern as Avery started in one direction, then turned back in frustration, uncertain and agitated.

"We need to find that blasted pub, the Goat and Gondola or whatever it was called." Avery's eyes were reduced to slits as he visibly appeared to be wrestling with some demon.

"The Goat and Dragon, old friend." Damien stood paralyzed by uncertainty. "You remember, of course, that it needs to find us, rather than the other way around."

"But we have to make the effort!" Avery choked on the idea. "We have to make the effort, or it will leave us in that same rigged booth that that chap occupied in that quiz program."

Damien had no idea what he was hearing.

Avery grasped his friend's lapels as he tried to regain some self-control, seeing the frightened look in Damien's eyes. "Sorry, old chap. But I am sure that *time is of the essence*, as some group of lawyers is fond of noting."

He began to breathe more regularly. The redness that had blossomed across his face receded slowly. "Time, acceleration, intention, motivation." He muttered these words as Damien looked on with increasing concern. "Where can we find that blasted pub? Don't you have any idea?"

In desperation, Damien pointed north along a narrow side street that was overhung by Elizabethan structures that wandered with medieval carelessness. "I don't remember that street before. It might just be that way." He felt helpless and terribly out of the know.

"Right! Let's away, dear friend, lest we lose all hope of catching up with the forces that seem to be gaining on us." His face contorted sadly. "I mean gaining on our world as we know it."

They hurried along the odd little street that quickly became hushed and pungent with antique odours: horse and cattle dung mixed with the unmistakable stench of human "slops." The only traffic was that of tumbrils and donkeys and horses. Avery grew agitated, and Damien felt as though they were entering the depths of the Underworld. Dogs barked, but there was no sign of Cerberus, the mythic protector of Hell, so he kept close behind Avery as he frantically searched for the pub he knew might be the only key to understanding the impending cataclysm.

"Don't you feel it, man?" Avery paused to take a sweeping survey of the time warp they had entered.

"Feel it, yes, and smell it, absolutely." Damien took a kerchief out of his breast pocket and covered his nose.

"Don't you get what is happening?" Avery took a wild-eyed look around. "We're being drawn back into history so that we can be slung out into the abyss, right through our time into the imperfect future that holds nothing but oblivion."

Damien didn't dare utter a word. He was too taken by the sensations of this place that both reeked of filth and hummed with the sad vibration of misery. His gaze went from the hobbled horses to the bent forms of humanity that made their weary way along the cobbled street. What was most eerie was the muffled restraint of sound. Wagon wheels made no more of a wail than the urchins trying to sell scraps of cloth they had doubtless found in some nearby dump. Suddenly he felt an urgent tug on his sleeve.

"There it is! Thank God, we've found it!" Avery was pointing to the now-familiar sign of the Goat and Dragon Publick House. "Quickly, lad, before we lose it and God knows what else." The two rushed through the swinging doors and let out a sigh of relief to find the interior unchanged from their last visit. Even Betty was there, dimly visible in the back. Faces turned their way then quietly returned to prior interests as though too embarrassed to take notice.

"Well come, gents." Betty's gravelly voice floated across the length of the room. "You have done well to find us at this point in time." She motioned for them to join her at the bar.

Avery gave Damien a wild look and nod of affirmation. "I told you, didn't I? Time is of the essence."

Damien followed his colleague, uncertain and increasingly ill at ease. His nostrils flared as the stench outside had permeated the pub, though he kept his kerchief in his pocket now.

"Whatever it is that you have come for, gentlemen, I fear you will not find it here." Betty spoke in a hushed voice that made both men extremely nervous. Her features were drawn and tense. Her eyes betrayed undiluted fear. "There is a force afield that answers to no man, not even to me." She peered at Avery as though he might reveal some key to the situation in the slant of his jaw.

Avery felt a strange sensation course over his face. He could see it was Betty's gaze that caused his flesh to trill and quiver as she searched for some secret sign that might explain her discomfort.

With a harsh clearing of her throat and a well-aimed expectoration, Betty sat back and frowned deeply. "I cannot tell whether you are the dupe of the devil or merely a specimen of your time." She ignored Damien and reached out to lay a shrivelled hand on Avery's forearm. "You have the vibrations of a normal human, but there is something else I sense. Something coming from afar." She withdrew her hand and turned to study Damien only for a brief moment. "And you carry the mark of the innocent—useless to any of us in this moment."

Damien said nothing, gladly waiting for Avery to find the words that might cast light on the situation. Tugging at his beard, Avery finally found his voice.

"The force that we have recently discovered, the one you know to have always existed, Mistress Betty, has somehow become aggravated, it would seem." He winced. "Whether it is the doings of those of us in science who have stirred up some ancient rage by our 'discoveries,' I cannot say. But, from all I have studied and learned just recently, there has been an unleashing of evil that this world has never before experienced."

Betty spat once more. "True and not true, if truth is what you seek." She cackled, and both men thought immediately of the witches at the outset of *Macbeth*. But for the lack of a cauldron, there sat the embodiment of superstitious mystery.

Avery's head began to spin. So much was vying for his limited means to cope. "You mean that what we face now has existed before? The world somehow survived a similar threat?"

Betty's face lit up. "Yes and no, Mr. Scientist." No cackle now, just squinted eyes and a dour mask seemingly carved from driftwood, grey and lifeless. Her gaze fell to study Avery's boots, a pair of fine British products, now stitched and shipped from China. "Your world has seen many twists and turns of late." She now fixed her eyes on his. "But what you have stirred up in the heavens is, as you suspect, beyond any threat to us all that I have known."

"Yes, but…" Avery had no clue as to what to ask.

"But, my dear sir, the ancient coming of the Great Darkness brought forth an understanding among my people that allowed the survivors to adapt, to…adopt even, some of the lessons learned." A wan smile quivered briefly.

Avery nodded. "I had a feeling that there was a close relationship between certain forces and your own powers, Betty. But you are saying that things are…different now? They are out of your control?"

Betty stared long and hard at Damien without responding, without blinking, lost in thought. Finally she turned back to Avery. "I have said that I have no influence over what is starting to happen. And I have said that the Great Darkness has come before. In many ways, it has never left this plane, only penetrated the heavens with its mysteries." She waved her hand broadly around the room. "All who have survived the original treacheries—those here who share my powers and you of the little world—are tainted with what Christians call 'original sin.' There is a trace, at least, of darkness in us all, a measure that is beyond redemption."

She turned again to Damien. "But there are some—a very few—who are borne of innocence without guile, without darkness deep within them, and they carry, I am told, the means to communicate with, though never control, the force of which you speak."

Avery stared with wonder, first at Betty, then at Damien. His features contorted into a kaleidoscope of emotions. Disbelief gave way to wonder. Uncertainty dissolved into joy. Finally hope beamed an uneven glow of warmth that quickly faded back to uncertainty. "What in hell are you trying to tell us?"

"A most telling choice of phrase, especially for a scientist." Betty raised a bony hand in rebuke. "I have just told you that hell dwells within each of us...or at least within most of us." She peered closely at Damien, as though he were a virus under a microscope. "I am reminded that there are such creatures as your friend here. They are very rare, and he is my first." She patted Damien's arm as though he were a child. She leaned in for a close examination of his features. "Yes, very rare." She shook her head, trying to remember an ancient saying. "I should have known..."

"What? What should you have known?" Avery practically fell off his stool as Damien sat with a growing sense of self-awareness.

Betty came out of a reverie. "Oh, just that there has always been a glimmer of light, something akin to the Greek legend of Cassandra's box that contained, in the end, that bitter residue of hope after all the virtues had fled." She cackled once more, a hollow, strident sound that seemed to come from another world. "Hope, Mr. Science Man, that feeds on itself until the bare bones of reality are all that remain." Her eyes swept from one man's to the other's, in a vain effort to stir unseen forces that might surface to identify themselves.

Avery felt a vague premonition spring from the back of his head. "Just a moment. You say that there has always been a glimmer of light, of hope, in the dull, dark annals of human history." He clenched his hands and stared at them, willing a dim recollection to take shape in his troubled mind.

"Not dull, Science Man. Never dull," whispered Betty, knowing that she didn't want to distract him from his task.

"There is so little to rely on," continued Avery, still lost in thought. His hands rose unconsciously to his chin, the fingers flexing up and down in syncopation with a growing awareness. "The world and darkness. Evil and light. Damnation and..." His features cleared, and he gazed at the dim surround of the pub. "This is nowhere, isn't it?"

"Always has been, yes." Betty nodded, a grin stirring her wrinkled chin.

"And where I come from is everywhere. Yes?"

75

"More or less, as you say." Betty continued to enjoy the moment.

"But"—Avery slowly let a hand fall toward Damien—"he is from another place."

"We call it another dimension, but yes, he is from another place." The entire pub had stopped to listen to this exchange now.

"And that other place, that other dimension, is one of light, of innocence, of...what?"

"Of the simple absence of what you Christians call sin. There are those who call it ignorance, blindness, dull wittedness. They are the ones who should know, of course, since they are the keepers of those very hobgoblins." She spat once more. "They can give some of us a bad name, you know?" A low murmur of amusement flooded the room.

Avery failed to conceal a pained look of doubt. He scratched at an eyebrow as he studied Damien's quiet countenance. "Why aren't you looking like the Cheshire Cat, old man, or at least the feline that ate the canary, eh?"

"I feel as though I've eaten a great deal more than a bloody canary, actually." Damien tried to look amused. "More like an ocean liner, from the feel of it."

Betty lurched on her stool. "Yes. Yes. So right! An ocean liner, indeed." She peered at Damien with renewed fascination. "It was the *Titanic* that triggered the great revulsion that spawned the Great War. You know, 'the war to end all wars.'" She let out a loud belch. "Such hypocrisy and self-delusion. And, as you know, such abject treachery."

Damien looked puzzled. "You mean to say that the launching of the 'unsinkable' *Titanic* brought on not only its own destruction but that of much of the Western world?"

"Very good, lad. Very good. There have been warnings throughout your history that, if ignored, trigger cataclysmic events. And, regular as clockwork, they are ignored. And the price is paid, and nothing is learned." She shook her head. "And it is not a matter of ignorance but wilful self-delusion." She threw up her hands and shrugged. "You—not *you* but your average humans"—she gave a dismissive nod to Avery—"are so vain and prideful that they cannot help but do themselves in."

Avery swallowed hard. "I would hope that—"

"That there is hope?" Betty appeared to float above her stool. She looked puzzled. "There is a phrase, the meaning of which I know not. *'Quod erat demonstrandum.'* I take it that you are familiar with this gibberish?"

"I…yes, I am familiar with that particular phrase." Avery looked quite embarrassed.

Betty looked far from satisfied. "Then we are in agreement?"

"About what, dear lady?" Avery turned to the silent figure of his friend with renewed consternation.

"About the irrelevance of your personal ambition." Betty scowled.

Damien finally broke his silence. "If it should please the court…" He caught himself, puzzled by what he had just said. "I mean, if I may get a word in edgewise, Professor Owens lacks any personal ambition in this matter, I assure you. He is merely acting on a gut feeling that the heavens are in tumult, or soon will be, and that he has a clue as to what is going on."

"You mean 'going wrong,' I trust, young man." Betty leaned back and tried to shake the image of a judge that she had adopted. "Do please elaborate, *Professor* Owens, as to your clue."

Avery grimaced. "This is, I believe, where our worlds diverge, even as they would benefit from teaming up." He noticed that the entire room was listening closely. "It is from my world, my perspective as a scientist, that I can see the possible link between what we call 'dark matter' and what we all agree is a destructive force that history has called evil. And that latter force is what you freely admit, madam, is part and parcel of your own world of deception and delusion. Am I right on that judgment?"

Betty gave a tentative nod and withheld comment.

"Ah, here come the ladies to my rescue." Avery jumped to his feet, all but sweating from relief as Fiona and Missy swept through the pub toward him. "Rather good timing, I must say. I shan't ask how you knew to come, of course."

Damien gave up his stool and moved down two seats as the ladies settled in with serious restraint etched on their features.

"As I have already tried to explain to these two"—Avery motioned toward the new arrivals—"the mere 'discovery' of dark matter by some of us in the scientific field appears to have stirred up a force that you, dear Betty, admit to not having witnessed in your lifetime." He paused, hoping for some correction or amendment from anyone there. Silence dictated that he continue. "Now, what would be of immense help would be if any of you knew how this force might be persuaded to cease and desist its apparent intent to engulf us all in its growing…animosity?"

Fiona was the first to speak. "Aren't you putting a bit too much personality into this force? I mean, how can you grant it the ability to feel animosity, for heaven's sake?"

"I can't. That is, I shouldn't. It's just that I have this gut feeling about… developments that I cannot rid myself of."

Missy raised a carefully etched eyebrow. "Surely you are proceeding on more than just a gut feeling."

Avery waved his hands in growing distress. "What else have I to go on? What else can I look to?"

Betty broke in. "He's right, of course. The destruction of my home is more than a gut feeling, and the stench of doom is as strong in my nostrils as it has ever been." She tilted her head reflectively. "More so." Her gaze took in the upturned faces around the room. Fear and uncertainty registered everywhere. "We are agreed that there is evil afoot, and if we might benefit from joining forces, so much the better, though I know not how that might help."

"Knowledge is power, or so it is said." Damien stirred uncomfortably on his stool. "And shared knowledge would be welcome, however it be wrought."

"Well spoken, young man." Betty patted Damien on the shoulder with her staff. "In numbers there can be strength, enough even to marry wiles and wisdom, science and superstition."

CHAPTER TEN

Inspector Graham stared at his pipe, lying lifeless in the old brass ashtray his late wife had given him for their fifth wedding anniversary. The paper he had written in college lay open under his folded hands as his mind tried to concentrate on the tobacco in the pipe. Uninvited thoughts would intrude as happy images of his school days would pop up, giving way to the blissful early years of his marriage. The comfortable surroundings of his home study gave him the peace of mind his life seldom allowed but held many distractions now that he was nearing retirement.

"Blast and double blast!" No hint of fire or even smoke rose from the scrutinized object. The inspector's head turned suddenly as the faint sound of laughter caught his attention. There was no one else in his snug three-storey home. His housekeeper had gone for the day. The maritime clock on the wall showed half past six. He mentally checked his schedule. No one was expected. Reluctantly he got up to see what he could find.

Opening the door to his study, he called out from what was the first-floor balcony. There was nothing but the rustle of wind outside as the streetlights went on and darkness receded from his doorstep. Then he caught it. The faint but distinct and unpleasant smell of sulphur. That was impossible, he knew, but his professional instinct had him rush to his desk and extract a vial from a lower drawer. He quickly opened the vial and swept along the balcony, stoppering it up again. The scent was all but gone by the time he had done this, but if nowhere else, it registered at the back of his brain and made the hair crawl on the back of his neck.

All he could think of was Leftenant Forsythe's report and the odd presence of the same smell at the destroyed home in north London; the house that had had no collateral damage to any neighbouring buildings. An impossible feat, from all the evidence, with a most unusual calling card. He returned to his desk and picked up the phone.

"Sorry to bother you at the witching hour, Leftenant," he paused, frowning. "But a most unusual thing just happened here that may throw light on that odd demolition piece you were working on." He instinctively looked back toward the now open door to his study. There was something there that was definitely undefined "You wouldn't care to come around for a drink, would you? Just to comfort an old man soon to be set out to pasture? Thanks awfully." He set down the phone and went back to investigate the hallway.

Minutes later, the doorbell rang, and Forsythe's unmistakable figure appeared like an apparition through the treated glass of the inspector's front door. With an unusual spring in his step, he descended the single flight of stairs to welcome his assistant. "Tell me if you smell anything peculiar, would you, Leftenant?" These words escaped before Graham had even greeted his guest.

Forsythe gave him an odd look but quickly strode into the front hallway with nose in the air and on full alert. She frowned and looked back at her boss. "Blimey! Sulphur, or I'm a blind mouse."

The inspector almost leaped in the air with excitement. "I have a sample right here." He waved the vial over his head but quickly calmed down. "Not that it will prove a thing, of course. What was I thinking? But..." He took Forsythe's coat after safely tucking the vial into his jacket pocket. "At least you and I know that there is something most peculiar going on, something that the chaps at headquarters may never catch onto." Again he paused as the enthusiasm drained from him.

"Not that that will prove anything, other than that there is another rascal in the pigpen, by the looks of things." Forsythe seemed elated. "What was that you said about drinks?"

"Where are my manners? The bar is just this way." He pushed his glasses down his nose and gave Forsythe a close look. "You do, or did, catch that odour, didn't you? That must be established before I lavish a glass of plonk on you, you understand."

"Most decidedly, Inspector, though I'm not sure that cheap red wine is quite what I had in mind." She allowed a warm smile that Graham had seldom seen in the office.

"Well…I suppose I can dig up a Pouilly-Fuissé for you, if it comes to that." Graham's spirits rose as he settled into the familiar jousting he and Forsythe often shared at work. But the severity of the mood returned quickly enough as he went to the kitchen and rummaged about in the icebox. "Nice vintage, they tell me." He straightened up with a wry smile, acknowledging his limited memory of dates, a recent failing.

"Any old year suits this girl's palate, thank you, Inspector." Forsythe followed her host to the pantry where he made a show of choosing a pair of fine crystal glasses. "Especially my favourite wine in such stunning goblets."

Comfortably seated in the drawing room, Graham raised his glass and hesitated. "To uncovering the truth about all these sulphurous goings on and hoping it is no more than a leaking gas main."

"I'm not sure I want to drink to a leaking gas main, though I suppose it is just a tad more odd than a Grecian urn, as long as it doesn't explode right under us." Forsythe's gaze swept appreciatively around the room, noting several obligatory photographs of the inspector with the usual suspects but also a careful selection of mementos from his wife's ventures into the souks of the day. "Lovely taste, your wife had. Cheers to her memory."

"Cheers, indeed. Thank you, Leftenant."

"Aren't we able to call me 'Sandy' in off-hours, Inspector?"

Graham looked appropriately uncomfortable. "Well, I suppose it won't go on the record, will it, Lef…whatever." He blushed and felt a quiver of the life force evaporating even as he sat. A flash of regrets about choices he had never dared take, the litany of foolish whims and follies, all paraded before him as he squirmed down, trying to dodge the converging consequences of age. "This may well be my last case, you know, so let's be sure and make it memorable, shall we?"

"I do hope you're wrong about the last-case scenario, but I suspect this could be rather a doozy, if my instincts are half on."

"Ah, hah! Now tell me what your instincts are letting on. I am most curious." He took a serious sip of his wine and tried to concentrate, something that had always come naturally until this moment.

Forsythe settled back, giving her glass a fond glance of appreciation. "I couldn't help but notice the topic of that paper you were going to bring home with you earlier. The one about the powers of the mind."

Graham grimaced. "Yes, it's just upstairs on my desk at this moment. A lot of poppycock, I'm afraid. I was quite young when I wrote that, after all."

"But it was the sixties, if my maths are correct, and there was a wide interest in all things paranormal at the time. Especially in the colleges."

"Yes, and here we are, fifty years on, and everything seems to have been debunked or forgotten—everything that we thought so important at the time, that is. It makes me begin to wonder what persists from generation to generation. What principles, what ethics, what beliefs in general survive from just my own youth?" He flinched from a deep-seated pain of uncertain origins. "It makes me, for the first time, begin to see the positive role of religion in the world, a role that I had always viewed with great suspicion before."

His guest took on a maternal glow of appreciation for this candour. "Why, Inspector, you are full of surprises. Who would have thought you to be an agnostic?"

"Hardly an agnostic, my dear…Sandy. More of a heathen, don't you know. A believer in the many manifestations that the ancient Greeks saw nature taking on, each with its own god or goddess." His eyes twinkled as his mind went back to the spirited debates in college that had helped to form his ideas. "There was nothing more powerful or remotely as important as Mother Nature for us then." His brow furrowed. "I sometimes wonder where that young fellow went, that fervent me who delighted in the mysteries and awe of Nature that we all worshipped."

"I suspect he is very much with us now, re-emerging as we speak." She raised her glass. "To the re-emergence of youth. May it blossom and prosper."

Graham eyed the young girl from over his spectacles and remembered why he had called her. "If there is one thing I need to keep about me, it is my wits. And I still need to hear from you what your thoughts on this whole matter are."

Forsythe nodded absentmindedly. "Of course. Of course. On to the theory that this young and clinically schooled mind has come up with." She pursed her lips. "The story going around the office is that the building in question, the one utterly destroyed by an unknown force, was the victim of an ancient curse." She raised a cautionary hand. "The last person out—and this was after the total collapse of the building—was an old hag who is reported to have magical powers."

"Then you mean that the building was brought down by the curse of an ancient person?"

"No, sir. You know how the boys at the office are. They put two and two together to get ten."

Graham scratched at his balding head. "Yes, of course they would, but—"

"They are bonkers, of course. But it did get me thinking about a variation of that theme, one that would acknowledge that the hag does have supernatural powers *but* that the destruction of her home was aimed at her, not done by her." She pretended to study the contents of her glass with acute concentration.

"What was this 'two plus two equals ten' comment you just made, Leftenant? And just who is bonkers, may I ask?"

Forsythe looked sheepish. "I know it takes a stretch, sir, but there really isn't any other explanation that fits any of the facts, as limited as they are. There are too many eye witnesses who swear that this woman is a full-blooded witch. You should see her picture! And without a single sign of explosives and with that persistent smell of sulphur, which you have just corroborated, in a manner of speaking, right here in your home, I submit that there are definitely devilish deeds afoot." Her eyes widened, as did her nostrils, and Graham felt a surge of energy he hadn't felt in years.

"Well, well. This does cast a different light on things, though I do suspect, and have for some time, that you are absolutely right about this." He held up a hand. "Don't quote me on that, not at least quite yet. If word should get out, this might be where they let me off, rather than let me sink my teeth into this one last case."

"Scout's honour." Forsythe raised her right hand with the appropriate fingers raised.

83

Graham set his glass down and studied his guest's features as though they were those of a stranger. "Forgive my staring...Sandy, but I hadn't realized that your eyes are green, just like my late wife's."

"Cat's eyes, they call them. A little brown and green thrown in. Yes, thank you for noticing, Inspector. I take that as a healthy sign that your youthful self is re-emerging, as we had hoped."

"There is certainly something there that reminds me of my youth all of a sudden. I am deeply indebted to you for that. It must be all this excitement about witches and devilish doings."

Forsythe sat forward, rather primly. "If we are right, and there has even been a whiff of things to come right here, then what the hell—if you will pardon the expression—do we do?"

"Excellent question, young lady." Graham rose to his feet and extended a hand to Forsythe. "If you will accompany me up to my study, we can see what evidence may present itself. Perhaps a stronger whiff of sulphur. Who knows?"

Stepping into the hallway, he barely suppressed a shout. The unmistakable aroma of his pipe tobacco was wafting down the stairs. With an expression of total disbelief, he turned to Forsythe.

"The hunt is on, young lady. We have contact. The impossible has happened." He took her by the hand, and the pair raced up the stairs. There, still sitting in its brass ashtray, was the inspector's pipe, emitting a solid column of smoke that swirled in rakish eddies as they entered the room.

"Well, I'm..." Graham caught himself, again feeling the presence that wasn't there. "That pipe was as lifeless as I felt just minutes before you arrived. Not a match was lit, not a..." He looked around and still couldn't throw the feeling that there was someone else in the study. "Do you feel anything odd? Sense any odours other than the tobacco?"

Again Forsythe's nose went into overdrive. "The natural musty smell of old books and your nasty habit of smoking...a little dust...have you a cat?"

"A cat? Good Lord, no. What would I be doing with a cat?" His puzzled features broke into a frown. "Funny you should ask that, now that I think of it. There was a large, extremely fierce-looking, feline at my front door just yesterday morning. As I reached down for the morning paper, the damned thing disappeared, and I assumed that it had shied away home. Do you think the little bugger could have gotten into the house?"

"I thought you said that it was a big bugger." Forsythe suppressed a smile as best she could.

"Yes, well, relatively speaking, big. And it had its back up, you know, and was snarling."

"I see. It sounds as though you are definitely not a cat person." Forsythe continued her perusal of the study with her nose. Choking on the smoke from the pipe, she had to give up. "Sorry. Allergies, you know."

Instinctively stuffing the pipe in his jacket pocket, Graham apologized profusely. "Terrible habit, isn't it?"

"Not worse than hiding it in your pocket, particularly if that is the pocket that contains the vial that contains the smoke that we both sensed before this little conflagration magically started up."

"Blast! You're so right. There shouldn't be any cross contamination, what with the stopper and all, but the way things are going...anything might happen."

Forsythe stood by the study door, waving the remnants of the smoke away from her, but couldn't tear herself away. "You're absolutely certain that you did not strike a match, possibly as I rang the doorbell and distracted you?"

"No possible way." Graham fumbled in his pockets and took quite a while to locate a book of matches in his watch pocket. "See. Practically unused. I swear. I may be losing it but not by that much."

Forsythe's face lit up. "Then we have a genuine case of spontaneous combustion spontaneously arrived at."

"I'm ever so glad that you are excited about all this, but, as you asked earlier, what the hell do we do?" Graham kicked at the bottom of his couch, but no cat emerged.

"What do you suggest in your paper there?" Forsythe nodded at the forgotten study lying on the desk.

"Oh, that. Let's see. What did I assume all those years ago?" He leafed through the stack of yellowed pages with something of a schoolboy's reluctance. "Yes, here's something." He cleared his throat. "'Contrary to firm belief in certain quarters, the powers of the mind can be found to channel certain energies with remarkable force. It is yet to be determined whether the energies in question are independent from external influences or are the sole result of individual effort.'" He took off his glasses to clean them and tried to hide a blush. "Rather bold, I thought at the time. And total drivel, when read today."

"Not at all." Forsythe could smell a clue, even from the door. "You were on to an important question that still hasn't been resolved, as far as I know. And that is one of causation, as they say in the classroom. In other words, who or what caused which reaction?"

Graham looked puzzled and grew increasingly uncomfortable. "You mean, the reason the pipe lit could have been because of my efforts, or it could have been by an external agency? And if so, what bloody agency?"

"I don't know about the blood, but I suspect, now more than ever, that the sulphur and the smoke…and the cat all add up to external agent or agents unknown and yet"—she looked carefully around the room—"very much linked together."

Two simultaneous sounds made them both jump from fear. One was the front doorbell going off with the impact of Big Ben, and the other was the sight and sound of a large cat bounding by the study door and racing down the stairs. "Great, galloping goldfish!" Graham managed.

"Looked more like a great, galloping cat to me, sir." Forsythe stood, gaping at the fleeing figure, as Graham rushed out to take in the scene himself.

"Now who the hell do you think that might be at my door at this hour?" Graham pulled out his pipe and instinctively shoved it in his mouth.

"I suspect we might try to be a bit circumspect about our language at this juncture, Inspector. Who knows? It might just be someone straight from hell out there, looking for her Pyewacket, her familiar."

"Her what?"

"Her familiar, sir. You remember the movie *Bell, Book and…*?"

"Oh, yes, of course. That beautiful girl with her cat in New York. Yes, yes. A familiar, yes. Well, let's see who it is looking for her…cat." He approached the front door with mixed emotions. "I don't suppose it could be anything like the girl in the movie."

Euripides sprang through the barely opened door and vanished behind the flared skirt of Betty from Bournemouth.

CHAPTER ELEVEN

Avery was trying hard to avoid having a panic attack. His scrupulous review of every scientific aspect of the facts as he saw them refused to add up. The theory that dark matter comprised the vast majority of the universe in order to keep it "glued together" seemed increasingly indefensible, if not obtuse. The theory that dark matter was composed of nonatomic particles, ones that escaped observation due to a lack of "substance," did ring true, as far as anything could that lacked proof of existence. But the kicker lay in the assumption that nonatomic particles could be "proven" only by their absence in a software dissection of the universe. This not only dictated the makeup of all things but did *not* have a moral or spiritual influence. He knew from what he had learned from Betty that that was far from likely.

He had learned from his strict religious upbringing that all things that sprang from the Creator—and that was virtually everything, down to the least sparrow—was part of the great mosaic of life and was inextricably interrelated. Even as he matured into a more secular humanist, the sacred links between the stars and life on earth remained just that, sacred. The popular notion that all things are made up of stardust only consolidated his beliefs. But it was solely in cheap horror movies that he had seen the link between darkness and evil so effectively portrayed. What did they know in Hollywood that he should be considering? What did science refuse to acknowledge that popular fiction could be so free to exploit?

The phone rang, and he was grateful for the diversion. Fiona's distinctive husky voice was on the line. Moments later he found himself hailing a cab and heading off to the site of Betty's former home. The ban on scavenging had been lifted, and there were artefacts to be gleaned. Why he was so excited by the prospect of noodling around in the wreckage was beyond him.

Furtive figures could be seen grazing through the remnants of their lives. The distinctive stooped form that followed the prowling of a large cat could not be mistaken.

"Hello there." Fiona waved from the edge of the property and pranced her way down to where Avery stood, paying the cabbie. "We thought you might know someone who could fix up Betty's telescope. She found it nearly unhurt, except a lens or two are broken. Just over there." She pointed to where Willy stood guard over a meagre pile of belongings that did include the vintage and valuable subject of Betty's nighttime vigils.

Visibly disappointed and quick to point out that he didn't know any repairmen in the telescope business, Avery nonetheless approached Willy with a strong sense of purpose. "Any further clues as to what caused this, Willy?"

A sullen look and a shake of the head was the sole reply. Willy kicked at the small heap of belongings his mother had been able to retrieve and slouched visibly. "Just a matter of too close for comfort, I guess."

"What does that mean? You got too close to whom…or to what?" Avery stumbled on a loose brick as he made the effort to shake Willy's hand.

Willy's features combined a deep pain and puzzlement as he briefly took in Avery's brightly inquisitive face. "Why, the force that my mother told you all about, of course. The one she'd never seen so pissed, so bloody minded."

Avery felt a strange tingle flow through his arm as Willy reluctantly shook his hand. "You wouldn't be a conductor for that force, would you Willy?" He shook his hand as it continued to feel as though an electrical charge of some magnitude had been sent through it.

"I wouldn't know anything about that now. I try to keep as far out of the way of any of that nonsense as I can." He called out to his mother who gave one last sweep of her eye across the ruins and made her way down to where Fiona met her and helped her across the last of the rubble.

"Well, Mr. Science Man, seeing is believing, as you might say." She swept her hair back out of her eyes and nodded toward the wreckage. "Not a stone left unturned and not a clue as to what might have caused it." She let out a crazed cackle and seemed genuinely amused.

Just then an official-looking black sedan pulled up with the markings of Scotland Yard barely visible on the driver's door. Inspector Graham and Leftenant Forsythe stepped out, and Betty found herself in the unexpected role of introducing everyone all around.

"The inspector was kind enough to find my cat the other day after the poor thing survived this horrible demolition and lost its wits." Euripides eyed everyone there and slunk off to look for rats. "And this kind gentleman," she said, nodding toward Avery, "has taken an interest in our retirement fund." She threw him a shrewd wink. "One that is more in need of help than ever, as you can imagine, Inspector."

The two younger ladies seemed genuinely interested in meeting, even as Fiona showed a pained restraint at the sight of a uniform. Sandy, for her part, immediately sensed a possible ally in her investigation and made a special effort to enlist Fiona, though as gently as possible. The upshot was that the group stood around for far longer than Betty wished to endure.

"Willy, you gather those things up and bring them along. Let the professor take the telescope to be fixed…and we just might let him use it a time or two for his troubles." A crinkly smile spread beneath dull eyes. "It would be worth your while, Mr. Science Man, I can assure you."

Avery took a closer look at the antique brass gateway to the stars. There was nothing that he could be sure of, but the feeling that something more than a telescope sat looking up at him was palpable. Even Graham cocked his head and wondered what it was that drew his attention so inexplicably to this relic. Betty saw the puzzled looks and gave her son a kick. "Come on there, boy. Do as you're told…out of respect for your dear old mother."

The group began to break up, but not before Sandy took down Fiona's phone number and the inspector exchanged cards with Avery. Promises were made to be in touch. Suspicions were laid to rest for the moment, and hope was the currency of the hour.

* * *

"My dear fellow, you aren't going to give me that old tripe about the star Wormwood, are you?" Inspector Graham was trying to engage in a meaningful conversation with Avery about the threat they both knew to be imminent, and passions were running high.

"Of course not. Though you shouldn't dismiss out of hand some of that 'tripe,' as you call it." Avery was having a hard time collecting his thoughts. There were so many concepts, theories, allusions, and uncertainties careening around his head that he was glad to be sitting down in a comfortable chair in the Inspector's club. "One thing I have learned over the years is that one should never dismiss any notion out of hand, Inspector. Even the seemingly psychotic, such as a wandering death star. Wasn't it Steve Jobs who said that only the psychotic survive?"

"I believe it was another one of those Silicon Valley chaps, and the expression was 'Only the paranoid survive.'" The inspector took brief refuge in his pipe, enjoying the billowing cloud that gave him a sense of invisibility, if not invincibility. "But you do have a point. We try to keep an open mind about most matters. It's just that there has to be a limit to what the system can bare."

"Don't I understand that, Inspector." Avery reached for the whiskey suspended on a tray by a well-tailored waiter at just the right height before him. "My system has achieved overload status long since, with no respite in sight."

"But you do think that the demolition of that Victorian domicile was done by…mysterious means?"

"Less mysterious, Inspector, than inexplicable, which, translated into the vernacular, reads 'bloody scary,' and that is an understatement."

A pained expression flooded the inspector's features. He bit down hard on his pipe and winced. "Damn, that's the second time this week."

He rubbed his jaw and tried to overlook the discomfort. "So you suspect that there is an occult force at work here?"

"I wish it were that simple. I mean, yes, an occult force, as you put it, but more than that, an alien presence the likes of which I don't believe we have seen before, at least not in modern history."

Graham continued to show signs of pain. "Worse than the Nazis? And the imperial designs of Japan?" His eyes darted about the room, trying to alight on some soothing object of reassurance. The bust of Britain's war-time prime minister scowled at him with just what he was looking for. "I can't believe the Yanks sent that take on dear old Winnie back to us. But I'm dimmed glad they did, aren't you? Just when we need a shot in the arm, or buttocks, who better to administer it than the spirit of Mr. Churchill?"

Avery followed Graham's gaze and nodded in quiet agreement. "If ever there was a time…" He nearly rose out of his chair in sheer disbelief. "That reminds me…of something I'm sure you have heard as well." He looked around at the staid surroundings and lowered his voice. "Surely you heard that Hitler delayed his plans to invade us due to the intervention by our valiant collection of…witches." This last word he barely whispered as Graham leaned forward to hear him.

"Oh, bollocks! Of course I heard that poppycock. But surely you don't believe any of that now?" Graham sat back in his chair and let out a worried blast of smoke. He had secretly been most proud of the possibility that his homeland security had, at least once upon a time, been administered by women who boiled up vats of bat wing and reptile parts.

"I not only believe it to be true, but it may be our best hope for survival, if my suspicions are accurate." Avery shook his head as he scanned the mostly older, comfortably dressed membership dotted around the room. Not a wizened old crone in sight, and these were the men who made all too many of the decisions on national policy. "What needs to be done is to bring old Betty in for a conference, don't you think? That would both alert the appropriate members of government to the situation and stir things up a bit." He couldn't help but grin at the thought.

Graham tried to ingest this suggestion without showing outright derision. Finally, he too broke into a smile of sorts. "Wouldn't that be memorable? I mean, you must be joking!" He couldn't suppress a laugh that came out as a loud gurgle that drew unwanted attention. "Can you imagine what the PM might say? He would have a cow right there on the floor." The imagery became too much, and he had to take refuge in his whiskey.

"Cow or no cow, something needs be done, and I can think of no better catalyst for the upcoming chemical reaction that seems sure as hell ahead than to stir old Betty into the mix and see what emerges."

CHAPTER TWELVE

Willy watched with a strange foreboding as Euripides stirred from a deep sleep, stretched, forming a cavernous, silent yawn and went to his box for a sustained evacuation of his bowels. The young Scot had to restrain himself from going over to inspect the results, half-expecting terrible portents to be evident in the fecal offerings. With singular indifference, Euripides yawned once more and went to sit in the sun streaming in the lone window that gave onto the street. Missy called out from the kitchen as she hurriedly fixed herself a bite to eat.

"Anything I can get for you before I disappear, Willy?" She poked her head into the living room and held her nose. "Oooh. Any chance you can look after that cat of your mother's?"

Willy remained silent for several moments before reluctantly unfolding his tall gangly frame from the sagging couch and approaching the cat box with acrid anticipation. "He'll shit all over all of us before this caper is done. Mark my words."

"Well, as long as we can clean it up before we all have to evacuate the premises, I suppose that is the best we can look forward to." Missy gave a halfhearted wave of her hand as she went through the door to the landing and gave a yelp as she nearly tripped over a neighbour's dog. "That hound will be the death of me yet," she muttered as she slammed the door and shot an icy stare at the dog's owner.

"Tony, haven't you and Thomas enough to do without tripping up poor neighbours?"

"His name is *John* Thomas, as if you didn't know, and come to think of it, no, we don't have a single blessed thing more important to do at any given time of day or night than make your life miserable." Tony made a face that fairly glowed with malice and morbid satisfaction. His slight build twisted from the knees up in what appeared to be an expression of joyous self-indulgence. But the smile that warped his lean mouth divulged the mirth behind the words. "You *are* such an easy target, and now that you have become an illicit boardinghouse keeper, there is no end to what John Thomas wants to do to you."

"My, I am so relieved to hear that." Missy tweaked the dog's ears and made a motion to do the same to its owner but galloped down the stairs instead. "Beware Euripides, Tony. That's all I have to say. Keep that dog of yours away from Betty's cat, or there will be hell to pay." The front door seemed to pivot as Missy passed through it and closed with a metallic thud.

Willy opened his door in hopes that something of interest was going on around him and immediately regretted the move. Fur was flying before either human had any idea what was going on. Snarls, yelps, and piercing sounds of pain tore through the building. Doors opened, and cries of consternation cascaded through the stairwell. Willy kicked at Euripides and landed a solid boot on its butt. Tony had instinctively dived to throw a protective arm around his dog's neck. Blood flowed from his wrist and quickly reddened his obviously expensive French-cuffed shirt. As Euripides bound back into Missy's flat, spitting and howling like a banshee, Tony stared at his arm as it turned an ever darker shade of red.

"We'd better get that looked at," Willy managed, still uncertain as to what had just transpired. He began to feel faint. Tony, a full foot shorter than Willy, now looked from his own injury to the ashen appearance of the Scot.

"You're not going to faint on me now, are you, you overgrown weasel?" Tony's agony quickly metamorphosed into indignation. He even drew strength from his growing pain, the discomfort feeding his sudden burst of irritation. "That fucking cat mauled my John Thomas. And look what it did to me!"

Willy felt more uneasy by the moment as the bloody arm was waved in his face. "We'd better get you round to the clinic before I fall over...I mean, before you catch an infection."

"How about 'before I bleed to death'? Look at me! Look at my shirt! It's ruined! Why, if I weren't a vegan, I'd chop that cat up and fricassee its backside till every hair on its balls fell out." Tony made a motion to go after the cat, which gave Willy the opportunity to grab him and stabilize his own precarious stance.

"Let's not be too hasty there, lad. You go after that cat, and there's no tellin' what the consequences might be." Willy waved a cautionary finger at Tony.

With a look that might have frozen over the sea, Tony stepped back, trying to determine just how mad this newcomer might be. "You're not trying to tell me that that cat has supernatural powers, are you?"

Willy scratched at his face for a moment, sensing an opportunity. "I am doing just that." He paused and nodded, enjoying the sensation of the words. "That cat"—he licked his lips in anticipation of some horrendous exaggeration—"can blow the face off the Sphinx, if it has a mind to."

Tony stooped to pick up his dog protectively. "In that case, I assume that you could blow the balls off a herd of charging bulls with just a twitch of your wrist."

Willy looked down at his wrist, wilted and limp from his condition. "You bet your prim little ass, buster." He began to recover his equilibrium. "And that's nothing compared to what my mum can do, be it charging bulls or prissy little neighbours."

Tony's knees instinctively merged before he threw his head back and spun round to retreat to his own flat. "We'll see who is prissy and who is pussy when my lawyers get through with your cat, mister. There's going to be more than damages it will be liable for, you can bet your scrawny soul on that."

There was nothing for Willy to do but slam his door and sulk back onto the couch with ever dimmer views of Euripides clouding his mind. With unpredictable precision, the cat bounded up onto Willy's lap and, for the first time ever, proceeded to circle and settle and purr. Astonishment gave way to puzzlement, then to a severe case of scepticism. A very tentative caress was greeted by ever-louder sounds of pleasure and claws driven into Willy's thighs with an odd pulsating rhythm. Nervousness gave way to a fuzzy sense of well-being, almost drug-like and intoxicating. The pain inflicted by the claws converted as it flowed to the brain into a sharpened clarity of mind. Elements in the room that had never before drawn notice suddenly became vivid, almost pulsating, with individuality. With the deliberation of a reptile, Willy's mind flickered around the cluttered room, noting first an ancient mask of unknown origins, then a pair of heads carved from the blackest ebony, a shield of obvious African heritage and a stone axe.

As Willy began to absorb the images of these objects into his deepest being, something he had never been aware of before, the door flew open. "What are you doing with my cat?" These angry words sent Euripides flying off Willy's lap in a sudden explosion of movement and sound. Ears laid back and tail high in the air, Euripides turned to confront Betty as she slammed the door behind her and seemed prepared to launch lightning bolts at anything that moved.

"How dare you steal my cat? How dare you interfere with him when my back is turned?" Betty stood like an ancient warrior, feet spread, one hand high over her head as though clutching a gleaming sword. "My only son now turned against me, are we?"

Willy was struck dumb. Not only had he experienced something far beyond his ken— thanks, he assumed, to the cat—but now he was launched into a dark, cold place that even his mother had never inflicted on him before. His mind kept wanting to reach out to the cat, to recapture the sense of what he realized had to have been companionship, even as he turned to face the meanness of his mother. "I don't know what...you can mean, mother. I had nothing to do with your cat coming to me. You know that. Euripides does what he wants." He swallowed hard. "It would seem as though he had a change in heart, or diet, or God knows what, but he wanted to share something with me, something that felt so incredibly grand and meaningful and important. And then you showed up. You broke the spell, Mother, like a jealous lover with a vindictive soul."

"We'll see who has a vindictive soul, you sad excuse for a human being. Euripides is mine, you understand, and mine alone. Without him, I am..." She hesitated, trying to parse a reasonable conclusion.

"You are what, Mother? Nothing? Is that what the truth is after all these years of your lavishing love and affection on that animal, instead of...anyone else?" Willy looked from his mother to the cat, who was still showing aggravated signs of aggression toward Betty. For the first time in his life, he felt more like kicking his mother than the cat. There was a twitch in his brain somewhere, an explosion of neurons creating the stimulating effect of serotonin that arced across his cranium and dove deep toward the reptilian core. His mother had never appeared so ugly, so haggard, so driven by bile and hatred. He didn't dare believe his eyes but knew nonetheless that he was witnessing a new layer of reality, a new version of what he had always taken for granted was the truth.

"I am never nothing, Son." Betty shook her head as she heard these words. "I mean, I have always been your mother, almost as long as I have had Euripides."

"But Mother, I am thirty-five years old. Are you telling me that that cat is older than I am?"

"Why, yes, Son, by a good bit, in fact." Betty tried to relax and advanced toward the couch, where Willy sank once more in despair. "Euripides was given me when I first…graduated from school, you might say. That same school where your cousin Hilary went, by the way." She raised her eyebrows in a knowing fashion and tried to smile. "She really hasn't done that well with her… studies after quite a promising beginning. Quite disappointing, actually."

"I suppose she can't even conjure up a vampire at will, or raise the dead." Willy frowned, listening to the inanity of his words.

Betty looked for a spittoon and let fly. "Come now, William Drury, you're not going to mock your old mother, now are you?"

Willy knew enough to stay silent.

* * *

Rufus and Charlotte were spending a rare evening in town. What was infinitely rarer was the fact that they were enjoying themselves. They were even enjoying each other. Neither had experienced anything like it, at least since puberty, and their delight was infectious. After dining at her favourite hotel, which he suddenly took a liking to as well, they decided to amble through the narrow winding streets that still bore the implacable mark of old London. The night sky took on a singular opalescent glow where gas lights still cast the only shadows along the way. The flickering effect from the dancing flames was all but hypnotic as they ventured down alleys they had never known existed. Entranced as they were with each other, they paid no mind to the distinct alteration of the scenes through which they passed. Sounds of merriment drew them around a precariously leaning corner to stop before the lead mullioned windows of the Goat and Dragon pub.

"How the hell did this place get here?" Rufus wound an arm around his wife's back as he peered through the windows.

"How the hell did we get here, is what I want to know," replied Charlotte, suddenly conscious of the odd nature of their surroundings. "Have you ever been by here, lovey? It all looks so…primitive."

"Even smells a little primitive, don't you think? It must be a movie set someone forgot to take down and the locals have just taken over." He glanced over his shoulder and gave Charlotte a wink. "Let's see what we can see, shall we?"

The crowd inside went silent as soon as the two were in the door. Curious faces turned up, then stooped low over mugs and glasses, trying to conceal the mixture of surprise and irritation that all there felt.

Neither Rufus nor Charlotte paid any mind to the sudden change in atmosphere. They were totally taken by the warmth and unusual vibrations each felt. The antiquity of the maps and engravings on the walls seemed so natural that neither gave them more than passing attention. The low, hand-carved beams could still be found in other locations but gave off an aura of lost times and intensity that quickened their pulses.

"Just the place for a nightcap, don't you think, darling?" Rufus spied an open table and hustled his wife to a waiting chair. As both sat and looked around with greater concentration, they realized that everyone there was uncomfortably aware of their presence. The silence that had met them at the door barely hummed now with the occasional whispered comment. Furtive glances shimmered through the room like fractured glass.

"What'll it be, folks?" A nondescript figure hovered with an unnatural lightness for the lumpen appearance and dishevelled attire that caught Charlotte's attention. "We don't serve folks what don't come from hereabouts, you understand?"

"Then why are you asking for our orders?" Charlotte peered up at the blank stare of the waiter with quick agitation. "It must be obvious"—she swept an elegant hand toward the crowded room—"that we are not locals."

"Yes, ma'am. I mean, no ma'am. It's just that you are here, you understand?" The waiter fumbled for words. "Something, I mean someone must have let you in, or you'd have passed us by." Bushy eyebrows raised in emphasis to this statement.

A nearby chair scraped back across the floor with embarrassed abruptness. "Do let me explain. May I join you? My name is Fiona Fairfax, one of the locals lucky enough to frequent our old, somewhat out-of-the-way public house."

Rufus jumped to his feet and pulled out a chair. "Do please join us. We would be delighted to understand why…it is that we are here. You do all seem a very tight-knit group, and we don't wish to intrude."

Fiona flashed a smile and settled into her chair, trying to find words that might clarify the issue. "We don't get many outside visitors here anymore." She tried unsuccessfully to hide her surprise. "We're frankly rather off the beaten path, as you might have noticed."

Rufus and Charlotte exchanged glances. "Yes, we did notice a difference about this neighbourhood that we had not sensed before." He held a hand out to cover Charlotte's. "But what is this thing about our being let in here?" He nodded at the waiter still hovering nearby.

"Oh, Charley just gets carried away sometimes, that's all." Fiona said something unintelligible to the waiter, who nodded and retreated toward the bar. "I've ordered you each a little cognac. I hope you don't mind the presumption?" She looked sharply at Charlotte and smiled. "One of our better vintages, not readily available elsewhere…"

"Oh my! A special reserve, Rufus dear. Does that remind you of something?" Charlotte's hand now curled up to enclose her husband's. "What a treat!"

Fiona took in the scene with an odd look of satisfaction as the waiter returned with snifters well filled with an amber concoction. "To your health, new friends, and to the appreciation of old ways."

Both glasses were raised as Fiona slipped her hand between the delicate orbs that Charlotte and Rufus had tried to click together. "Those, too, are very old. You'd be surprised how many we lose to the exuberance of the moment."

Rufus tool time to admire his gift. "Handblown, by jiggers. Beautiful! And what, may I ask, is the vintage?"

"Something like 1832, I believe. A good year, I am told." Fiona beamed as her guests gushed over their good fortune. But then came the moment all others in the room were waiting for. "Now that you have tasted of our hospitality, what is it that has brought you here?"

Rufus and Charlotte exchanged puzzled glances. Each began to feel the warmth of the brandy course through their veins and lighten their spirits even beyond their earlier joy. At the same time, there was a growing sense of uncertainty, of wariness, of loss of control. "Why," Charlotte began uncertainly, "we just wanted to enjoy the evening with a bit of exploration and a walk."

"We haven't done this before, actually," Rufus continued. "We are a bit new at all this romantic business, you know." He blushed as he realized that he had never been so candid in his life.

Fiona raised a hand, paused, and let it drop as she processed this information. She briefly caught the gaze of several others around the room, each of whom seemed certain as to the consequences of what they had just heard. Fixing Rufus with a now steely eye, she reached out to touch his hand. The vibration she felt was just what she suspected. Nodding to all in the room, she allowed herself a smug look that could only be interpreted as one of great discovery.

"You both are welcome to our little corner of the world," she began, looking to the front door as it was flung open and the anxious face of Betty materialized with a flourish. "And indeed are most timely in your appearance."

Murmurs swelled behind Betty like shock waves as she advanced toward the newcomers, who peered at her with a strange glow of recognition spreading across their faces. Betty stopped to survey the scene, staff in hand like an ancient wizard, and nodded in satisfaction. "I see we have guests, newly arrived from...elsewhere who need proper indoctrination." She sat with a smooth motion that belied her age and studied each of the new faces with maternalistic care.

"They were out on a stroll, Betty, new lovers with not a worry in the world." Fiona made the introductions as Betty's presence all but mesmerized Rufus and Charlotte.

Charlotte came out of her apparent trance long enough to explain that she and Rufus had been married for some time but had only recently really fallen in love.

Betty just sat there, noting the brandy and the nearly rhapsodic looks on the newcomers' faces. She then briefly turned to Fiona and muttered a whispered comment. When Fiona replied in the affirmative, she sat back and worked her hands together in a warming motion. "Well, my lovelies, it was so nice of you to drop by. We were in need of some…help in a little experiment that we thought would be good fun to try." She cocked her head. "Are you willing to try a little trip into the unknown for us? It would be ever so helpful to us all if you would."

The two nodded in unison, and Betty shot a knowing glare at Charley who reached into a cabinet and carefully extracted a small decanter. Several moments passed as he searched for the appropriate glasses, and Betty tried to contain her impatience with small talk. "You are so good to an old woman to help out this way. You seem to be just the type we were looking for, all rapture and innocence, unlike the lot of us here who…never mind." Her eyes widened as Charley set down the tray with the decanter and just two glasses.

"Are you not joining us?" Rufus raised his glass and seemed interested only in its contents, even as he made the effort to be polite.

"No, no. We're all old hands at this little trick." Betty kept rubbing her hands together. "We need new blood for anything interesting to happen." She made a lame effort to smile. "And your blood…I mean you both seem such nice people, just the type we were looking for."

Both Rufus and Charlotte seemed oblivious to any threat. They sat holding hands and swaying slightly as the effects of the new concoction began to take effect. Betty pulled her chair in close as they closed their eyes and began to nod as though adrift on a friendly sea.

"Just pretend that you are sitting at your favourite table in your favourite room of your favourite place." She leaned forward to monitor their breathing. "It's a cloudless day, with the sun about to set, shining bright into your eyes." Betty pursed her lips a she saw their eyelids quiver. "Bright, bright sun lowering to the horizon faster and faster." Rufus and Charlotte both threw their heads back in unison. "Now the light falls through the sky, and darkness comes." Both heads fell forward and hung as though slumbering. "And now you both can hear the sounds of the stars—distant,

101

shrill, calling." A convulsive twitch began to manifest itself in both bodies as their hands clutched and squirmed and then lay still. "You are falling now, from the farthest star back toward earth. There is a terrible silence that has clutched you in its grip. There is a void that wants to swallow you both as you hurtle by. There is darkness, nothing but darkness now."

The entire room was silent as Betty pronounced each condition. Fiona sat back as far from the couple as she could while her gaze remained riveted to their every move. This was just a simple experiment, she knew, but the implications could be enormous. If these two could survive a trip through layers of space that her kind took years of preparation to manoeuvre successfully, then there was proof that there was fallibility in all their precepts. Or that there was sure evidence of changes taking place that rendered their whole world obsolete. She barely resisted the temptation to let out a shriek that might break the spell on the two outsiders, an act that could find her falling through the darkness herself, lost beyond the pale of forgiveness or redemption. And then, to her horror, she heard it. A shrill cry that could have come from nowhere but her own throat. She watched with growing agony as the couple beside her turned grey and still.

Betty let loose a loud curse. "Damn you, woman. You have ruined all." She raised her staff and struck Fiona across the back of her neck. "You must pay, even as these two have paid." She gave each a poke, but knew there would be no response. "They must be removed…No, wait. They may be of help yet. Put them in the freezer, Charley. There may be a role for them to play before this game is done." She glared across the room at no one in particular before settling back in her chair to confront Fiona. "At least they can vanish without a trace, my dear. You…you may find yourself in quite a different set of circumstances."

CHAPTER THIRTEEN

Inspector Graham was having a hard time with his tie. "Dammit, I knew I needed a simple clip-on version. Doris was the only one who ever managed to get this right." He had lamented the loss of his wife as little as possible, but moments like this were unavoidable. His mind wandered involuntarily back to happier times, moments he began to realize that were marked more by the lack of aches and pains than by true happiness. He grimaced as he tried once more to convince his mirror that he could do the job. He banished the thought that life had been easier because there was less sinew and tendon insinuating itself into his life. A smile briefly dispelled the clouded scowl at his incompetence. "Sinew insinuating." Not bad for an old fart, he had to admit.

The doorbell sounded, and he knew he was running late. Leftenant Forsythe had thought it quite "modern" to stop by his place for their first official date, one made much easier for Graham since Owens would be joining them later as a chaperone, or so the joke went. Grabbing his jacket and fumbling with the light switch, the inspector made his way down the stairs as swiftly as he dared and carefully opened the door.

"My, you are looking smart." His wife had drilled into him the need to observe the obvious. "Let me just call for a taxi, and we will be off."

"I thought a bit of a walk might be in order, what with the weather cooperating, the cost of cabs so obscene, and the restaurant being so nearby." Forsythe grinned, and the evening sky illuminated a face so alive with wit and intelligence that Graham found himself staring.

"Well, I must say, if they take me off the force for intraoffice dating, I shan't be the least concerned." He resisted the opportunity to give her a peck on the cheek, even though she seemed to expect it. Turning to lock the door behind him, he dropped his keys.

With the swiftness of a cat, Forsythe stooped and retrieved them. Rolling his eyes, Graham bowed in gratitude and managed not to make another blunder all the way to the restaurant. Small talk seemed to come far more lightly than he ever imagined. His companion's ease and natural composure dispelled his nervousness and natural reserve. Halfway through dinner, he even began to wish he hadn't invited Owens by for coffee and brandy.

"This is too good of you...Sandy, to put up with an old man with such apparent pleasure. But now that we have such personal idle talk behind us, I would like to get on to business, if you wouldn't mind." He wiped his mouth with as stern a move as he could muster at the moment.

"As you wish, sir." Forsythe seemed quite primed for the job. Adopting a prim attitude as she straightened herself in the comfortable banquet where they had lost themselves to personal whimsy, she took out her iPhone and studied it for several moments. "The official conclusion about the cause of destruction to the domicile in question is still under debate." She grimaced. "The Yanks have their knickers in a knot over the possibility of some supersecret explosive device that they envision being used on their public transport system."

Graham nodded and tried to keep his personal thoughts to himself. "When they catch on to what happened on 9/11, they can really get exercised," he muttered. He straightened up. "That's off the record, of course, Leftenant."

"I assume that all of this is off the record, sir." She reached for her wine glass and drained the last few drops. "Now there are some of our lads—rural chaps, for the most part, if you know what I mean—who are convinced that it's the work of the devil...or at least a good variation on the diabolical." She raised an eyebrow but wasn't about to comment further.

"Well, bloody hell. What else can a sane individual come up with?" Graham raised both eyebrows and wished Avery would appear. "I mean to say, Sandy, that there is no evidence to the contrary, and when there is no evidence to the contrary, the obvious, however surreal, must be taken seriously." He looked in vain for Avery's approaching figure. "If it weren't for that cat and the burning pipe and Owens' theories and that old hag, I might be a bit more sceptical, but…please. Ah, there you are. Nothing like being a bit tardy to get the evening off to a bang, eh, Owens?

Apologies, excuses, and general banter ensued. But only briefly.

"What's the latest, eh, professor?" They all pretended to concentrate on their desserts.

"Precious little, I'm afraid, except…" Avery tried to suppress a look of triumph. "We got the strangest reading last night. Totally different but tantalizingly decipherable." He sat back and studied the two faces upturned with intensity. "There was what we call an abnormality in the night sky." He cleared his throat. "By that I mean something—"

"Weird." Forsythe couldn't contain herself. She quickly glanced at Graham to judge his reaction, then leaned intently toward Avery. "Please forgive me. You were saying?"

"Yes. Of course you are forgiven, especially as you are spot on. 'Weird' fits the description as well as any word." He poked at his dessert, trying to seem calm. "There was an intrusion, an object or objects that penetrated the full spectrum of our atmosphere."

Graham frowned. "But, my dear chap, that happens quite frequently, I thought. You know…meteorites and that sort of thing."

Avery tried to keep a straight face. "Of course, but this went both down and, first, went up." He looked at each of his listeners with the lost composure of a twelve-year-old. "Up, then down, and with the speed that outdoes any rocket that I know of, *and* it was launched from right here in the middle of the city."

The three of them just sat and tried to digest the possibilities. "I have tried to make contact with the Home Office and the defence chaps to see what they know, but they are either playing dumb or are, in fact, out of the loop on this." Avery shrugged and shook his head as he trowelled in a large mouthful of tiramisu.

Graham looked over at Forsythe and felt ill. His face obviously showed his emotion. "What else have you got for us, dear boy? Anything cheery, just by chance?"

Avery recovered from his gluttony. "It does appear to bear out certain theories that I have been trying to enunciate for so long, and it throws some light on other possibilities beyond basic physics. Our spectroscope picked up vibrations, or frequencies, that denoted cellular life—living organisms. So this was not just a spaceship or meteor but actual living tissue that somehow outmanoeuvred all the thousand natural shocks that flesh lies heir to in our atmosphere and above." He shifted uncomfortably in his posture. "As you know, under normal circumstances most everything burns up travelling at any speed through the earth's protective shield. So for this 'traveller,' as I will call it, to avoid annihilation, there must have been a protective device or—for lack of a better word—spell that allowed it to traverse the heavens with such speed and force." He adjusted his glasses. "Any questions?"

Both Graham and Forsythe sat in a state of shock, but the latter soon rallied. "How can you possibly know that this 'traveller' was a living being?"

Avery winced. "Our equipment is fairly outdated, but there have been means to measure frequencies for years now, frequencies that translate into various materials, even flesh."

Graham sat back with a sudden sigh of relief. "You know, this all makes me glad I am as old as I am. I'm not programmed for all this modern wizardry that you chaps seem so comfortable with. But," he said, raising a triumphant hand, "I do believe I am just old enough to pick up on the importance of your use of the word *force*."

Avery gave a quick nod of appreciation. "Very good, Inspector. *Force* is the key word here as it is the singular element that makes any and all movement possible." He rolled his eyes. "Without either going into quantum physics or recalling our elementary lessons on heat transfer, what we are dealing with in all our investigations is the application of force beyond current understanding—whether it is the device that destroyed Betty's home or propelled this 'traveller' through space or…threatens us all in ways we can only imagine."

"So, come on man, give us your conclusions." The inspector was feeling unusually spry for that time of the evening. He laid a hand on Forsythe's outstretched arm.

Avery grimaced. "As I have said, there is no concrete evidence that any of my theories are valid, but"—he grinned—"there is increasingly little evidence to the contrary."

"Spoken like a true Welshman." Graham reluctantly withdrew his hand from his date's arm. "I will make every effort to get through to some-one—if he or she exists—who knows anything about all this at the Home Office. And Sandy—I mean Leftenant—if you would make what inroads you can at Defense. Use that charm of yours with those addlepated blokes in uniform and report back…Now just a minute. This isn't a top secret conference. My apologies, my dear." He cleared his throat. "If and when you have the opportunity to hop around to the Ministry and chat up some chaps, it would be ever so much appreciated if you would get back to me at your earliest convenience." He rubbed his hands together vigorously at the very thought of such restraint.

Forsythe gave him a knowing look of admiration, a warm smile illuminating her fair features. Then she turned back to Avery. "I don't quite get the connection between your theories on dark matter and the situation as we see it now."

Avery looked quite embarrassed. "My dear, it is elementary, and I mean that quite literally. It is the elements that dictate the rules, we have discovered, not those of us who think we are in charge. It is not those of us who push buttons and own gadgets who make a difference." He suppressed a smile of revelation beneath his beard. "It is those who are in league with Nature, who understand the vagaries of atomic mass, who can, in effect, cast spells, who control our future, for they are on an intimate basis with the elements. They respect all matter as it exists. They are not bound to change or bend Nature to their will. They live in harmony with what they find and can apparently learn from that better than the rest of us." He spread his hands in sheer dismay.

"And the 'they' you speak of are…?" Forsythe was bursting with curiosity.

"Why, our very own legions of witches, of course." Avery adjusted his glasses with a sense of glee. "Britain boasts more witches per capita than any other country in the world. If you think that old crone, Betty, is anything but, you should really consider another line of endeavour." A split-second smile creased his features. "And even if she is not at the centre of what's going on, I do believe that we should be able to learn a lot by keeping a close eye on her and any of her kind."

"I suspect that that idea of yours of introducing Betty to some members of Her Majesty's Government might be in order, eh, old man?" Graham winked at Forsythe as he asked this deadly serious question.

"I'm not at all sure what good it might do. After all, it does seem as though a prerequisite for serving in our government is to be as obtuse as possible." Avery looked as despondent as he felt.

"Now, now, I do know what you mean, but there are exceptions even to that rule, after all." Graham fought the inclination to be dour and even felt a surge of energy that didn't derive entirely from being so close to his aide. There was an odd sense of excitement that he was about to share an experience that would make all the recent aches and pains of aging disappear in a flash or at least in a wave of new beginnings.

He looked across the table and around the sumptuous room. There was a hum, a vibration, he was picking up that he noticed no one else seemed aware of. He dared to seek out Forsythe's attention by once more placing his hand on her arm. The reaction he felt, more than saw, was one of warm sharing, of affection and of trust. "I'll get going on setting up a meeting between Betty and some poor miserable unsuspecting soul at Whitehall, then. We can see where things go from there and possibly even profit more than a cheap thrill from the clash of cultures."

Forsythe dabbed demurely at her mouth with her napkin. "I wouldn't count on too much cooperation from the lady from Bournemouth if I were you, gentlemen."

A sudden silence fell. "Splendid point, Sandy, lass." Graham nearly choked. "You ladies are a mysterious lot that we poor blokes have to try to decipher mood after mood, world without end."

Raised eyebrows from both Avery and Sandy caused a wash of red to flood Graham's features. "Now whatever made me say that, I wonder? I do apologize, dear lady, for the totally tactless comment." He shook his head and frowned. "I know there's something in the air—and I don't mean that literally—but there is no excuse for old-world gender benders in this day and age."

"Apology accepted. Thank you, sir. Point made and filed." Forsythe's back reverted to its earlier resemblance to a ramrod.

* * *

"What? You expect me to go and talk before some magistrate at Westminster?" Betty's face was a study in geologic shift, creased with disbelief one moment and scarred by tremors of mirth the next.

"Not a magistrate, exactly. More a public servant, a chap who gathers information…" Graham was glad Forsythe hadn't accompanied him on this mission.

Betty gathered her skirt around her as though rodents might crawl under at any moment. "You mean a spy, some bloke what takes your name and puts it in a computer?"

"Well, I suppose they do that to all of us these days, now don't they?" Graham was suddenly wishing he did have Forsythe with him.

"Not me, they don't! I keeps my business to myself, and I got no quarrel with any sot what gathers taxes." Betty squinted at the inspector and paused, her nose suddenly quivering like a rabbit's. "You got problems, mister?"

"I should hope not. What sort of problems?"

Betty's eyes remained a blank void of information. "'Twasn't nothin'." She enjoyed playing the fool when confronted by any authorities.

Graham shifted uncomfortably on his makeshift seat on a kitchen stool in the flat that Betty now called home. Missy and Fiona watched from the sitting room while Willy tried to entice Euripides into sitting on his lap again. "If I could just convey the importance that your meeting with this gentleman might mean to…your country, Mrs.—"

"Name's Betty. No missus. Never got married." She nodded toward Willy. "That one just came along unbid. Why, I'm so old, I don't even remember my family name anyhow. What difference does it make anyway?" She was getting annoyed and enjoying it. "And what's this nonsense about 'my country'? It hasn't felt like my country since…Boadicea was a girl."

"Now, correct my memory…"

"Gor' blimey! You don't know who Boadicea was?"

"Oh yes, of course." Graham rolled his eyes. "She was the head of the barbarian hordes here in Britain at the time of the Roman invasion, wasn't she? How stupid of me. I walk by her statue often enough there at the bridge, driving all those wild horses. Most impressive!" He sighed, knowing he had dodged a bullet all too closely.

"More impressive than you might think, Mr. Inspector, far more impressive…" Betty fumbled with a purse she had in her lap.

"I am so glad that you mentioned that sterling example of a woman who so valiantly defended her country." Graham thought he might have hit on a favourable tack. "What we would like you to do is to follow in that honourable tradition set by Boadicea all those centuries ago, to come to the defense of this emerald isle that we all call home." He paused to hear what he felt had to be favourable reverberations in his head.

Betty glanced toward the two ladies waiting quietly in the next room. They seemed to communicate without the slightest need for sound or body movement. "Well," she concluded, "if you're going to put it that way, why I would be happy to follow in the footprints of our spiritual leader, Boadicea." She suppressed a grin, barely.

Graham was too delighted at the pronouncement to bother deciphering what had actually been said. "Splendid! That's just what we need to hear. I'll set things up, and we'll be in touch." He stood, feeling oddly shaky but dismissed the sensation as either euphoria or old age.

CHAPTER FOURTEEN

The bobbies at the entrance to Whitehall were more curious than courteous. As Betty neared their security post, closely accompanied by both Inspector Graham and Leftenant Forsythe, she drew both attention and stifled comment. Her staff was quickly seized and passed around amongst the puzzled group. When asked to raise her arms for a female guard to frisk her, she almost turned and ran. Had she been able to grab her staff and flee, she surely would have, but excruciating moments later, she was free to advance up the historic marble staircase to the warren of offices that lie at the heart of Britain's governing system.

"It tells a lot about what a sorry bunch this is when they don't allow an old woman her walking stick." She seemed to be having less trouble than Graham, and even Forsythe, in climbing the stairs. Her eyes darted everywhere, taking in the intricate carving of stone and ancient wood along the way and the smartly dressed guards stationed every few yards, it seemed.

"I believe they hadn't seen anything quite like your 'walking stick,' as you call it. And besides, they would have taken such a potential weapon away even from me had I brought it." Graham hoped that someone might detect some secret substance or clue to magical applications while they were upstairs but doubted his luck. There was an unusual amount of communication going on between the guards as they proceeded, and Betty couldn't resist a comment.

"Seems they all have some itch at the wrist they are trying to bite off, don't it?" She managed to convert a sneer into a snarl as she watched the odd behaviour preceding them down the hallway.

"It rather looks as though they are expecting some potentate to come along," Graham allowed, turning to see who might be following them.

"I do believe it's us, sir," Forsythe managed, getting a kick out of the relative commotion. "I heard at the office that someone was going to tip off the crowd down here that Betty was…to be watched."

"Dammit, Leftenant. You might have told me that. The minister is likely to be out by the time we get to his office, if what you say is true." Graham checked his watch to see that they were minutes behind schedule. He was all too aware what that might mean. "I have a terrible feeling…"

"Now, now, Inspector. You should have more confidence in your fellow minions in the national morass you call government." Betty cocked an eye up at the troubled Graham and touched his sleeve. "Believe an old crone when she tells you that there is no one in this building who doesn't wish to speak to me." She cackled, heard the echoes, and laughed out loud.

There was what appeared to be a footman waiting at the appropriate door. He bowed as Betty swept into the outer office of what seemed to be a secondary minister's assistant's reception room. Graham couldn't be but impressed. The only other time he had seen such respect shown was when he happened to be with one of the royals. His raised eyebrows spoke volumes to Forsythe, who was quite enjoying herself.

"The minister will be with you shortly." This from an earnest young man who couldn't keep his eyes off Betty.

Everyone sat down as Betty continued to take in every detail of her surroundings. Graham was impressed by the fact that she seemed quite at ease, even eager to get on with whatever lay ahead. A smile had crept across her face and now seemed etched there.

"Have you any idea, Inspector…? Yes, I'm sure you have." Betty's gaze continued to wander.

"Any idea about what, Mistress Betty?"

"Oh, just the colossal accumulation of wasteful thought that has seen the light of day in these offices. The odour of their ill-begotten birthing shall not soon perish from the earth."

Both Graham and Forsythe sat up at that phrasing. Each caught a glimpse of a twitch on Betty's face that seemed to come from the grave. There was a hollowness to her voice, a resonance neither had heard before. Just then the inner door opened with some diminishing caution and out stepped a far higher-ranking member of Her Majesty's Government than Graham had expected.

"Well, well," the minister began as two others stepped out from behind him. "This is a most unusual moment, I believe, for all of us." He moved quickly to sit behind a large modern desk and motioned for everyone to sit as well. Betty's taking sure aim at a spittoon that somehow sat by the minister's desk quickly dispelled the discomfort of the moment. "Well done, madam. I believe that is the first time that object has been properly used since the war."

Betty nodded. "Glad to see this place has some comforts of home."

Introductions were not made in spite of the formality of the meeting, a point not lost on either Graham or Forsythe. Anonymity seemed the order of the day, to the extent it could be kept. The two men behind the minister were vaguely familiar to the inspector, shadowy denizens of the intelligence community.

"Shall we get right to the point," the minister began, clearing his throat and shuffling a stack of papers that appeared to have some relevance to the moment. "We understand, madam, that you have some information that you wish to share with us." Spectacles were pushed up a bulbous nose to partially conceal a pair of small, dark, inquisitive eyes.

Betty let out a grunt and turned abruptly to Graham. "What's this now? I wasn't told I had to bear witness to nothing, nor even speak, if the whim don't itch."

As all present were taken aback, Graham responded as best he could. "My dear la...Betty, you didn't expect to be just gazed at as a stone-silent piece of evidence. Now, please be reasonable."

"Reasonable? I wants me rights—that what I wants. Nothing more." Her face glowed with a sense of resentment, but a foot darted out from under her skirt as a sure sign that she was enjoying herself.

"My dear madam, we are here to ensure you that you have all your rights...and then some." The minister looked from Graham to Betty and then to his stack of papers with obvious discomfort. Just then the phone on the desk sounded. The minister quickly took a message and hung up, his round face seeming to turn to stone. "I'm a busy man, madam, and we would like to get a few things straight. That's all."

"Well, what's in it for me, mister? I can get most anything straight there is, but it takes a little"—she extended a hand with fingers working together—"encouragement, it does."

Graham anticipated the minister's displeasure. "Betty, how dare you speak that way to a member of Her Majesty's Government? May I apologize, minister, for that unfortunate outburst?"

"It's quite all right, Inspector. I believe the lady and I understand one another." The minister turned briefly to mumble something to the two behind him, then pulled his chair in officiously close to the desk.

Graham anticipated Betty's denial of being a lady and gave her a nudge which, interestingly enough, got no reaction from her. Forsythe just looked on, taking mental notes prodigiously.

"We have a situation, madam, that requires some elucidation from you, if possible, or from the inspector, if necessary. It pertains to the destruction of your home and that of several others, and the persistent rumours that there are evil spirits abroad." He sat back, looking as though he had just swallowed a frog.

Betty's eyes lit up. "Evil spirits, is it?" She cocked her head and winked at Forsythe, who beamed back with anticipation. She took a long moment, gazing at her lap, then levelled her stare at the minister. "I wish there was a time when there were *no* evil spirits abroad, Mr. Government Man. But you're right. There are things what I cannot explain, and you can imagine…" She raised her eyebrows and flared her nostrils. "If I can't explain 'em, then there is potential hell to pay, if you'll pardon the expression."

"Just what we feared," exclaimed the minister. "All too well-chosen words, madam. Hell is just the sort of payment we were hoping to avoid." He briefly turned back toward the other two behind him. "We would dearly like to know the extent of the threat that we might be facing and where it might be coming from." A bead of sweat started down his forehead, which he ignored as he stared with a twitching eye at Betty.

Betty put a hand to her mouth, her attention briefly wandering. "Where might it be coming from?" She choked off a laugh and took aim at the spittoon once more. She waved a hand abstractly in the air. "It will come from just where the Scarlet Pimpernel did come from. Here, there, and everywhere." She cackled as she saw the minister squirm with discomfort and the other two roll their eyes.

"I see." The minister sat forward. "At least you do admit that there is a threat to the country and that it is imminent…coming possibly soon?"

Betty chose to remain silent. It was difficult to tell if she were about to clam up entirely or to let loose with a broadside of information. Graham crossed his fingers, and Forsythe held her breath.

"Let me put it this way, Mr. Minister. If the force that took down my home was to get riled up enough at your little empire, with all the bricks and marble that hold it together, you wouldn't last a minute." She pursed her lips as though tasting bitter fruit. "Make that an hour." She nudged Graham at that attempt at humour.

The minister swallowed hard. "And how would that all come about, may I ask? What form does this force take?" The three inquisitors leaned forward, quizzical looks creasing each of their pallid faces.

Betty shot a brief glance at Graham and Forsythe. Again, she hesitated, fumbling for words, it seemed, or debating whether to reveal all she knew. It was hard to tell. "You have to know that I am not sure just what is happening 'out there.' There is a gentleman who says he is a scientist—known to these two—who thinks that the barrier between our world and yours has broken down. He thinks that what he calls 'dark matter' is going rogue, he does."

Notes were hastily scribbled. "Does he say what this 'dark matter' is composed of?" The minister looked anxiously from Betty to Graham and back again.

"Gor' blimey! Don't ask this old woman." Betty nodded toward the inspector. "Ask him what it all means before you ask me."

Graham shook his head as the minister's gaze fell on him. "There are growing theories, Minister, but nothing concrete as yet."

"Hah. 'Concrete.' That's a good one." Betty hunched forward in silent disdain after that.

"We are aware of the theories you cite, Inspector…those of a Professor Owens, am I right?" There was a brief moment of self-satisfaction before a tremor of discomfort returned to the minister's right hand. "What we are curious about at this moment is the testimony of this…woman concerning the threat to national security that these sinister forces might hold."

Betty sat back and squinted. "Lord love us, dearie. I've already told you that the threat exists and that as far as I can see, there is nothing that anyone can do about it, not even my...kind."

"So these forces are not a manifestation of what your kind normally tap for your ceremonies and incantations and spells?" The question was posed without the slightest hint of sarcasm.

Betty cocked an eyebrow and shook her head.

"And you swear that you had nothing to do with the destruction of your home? And furthermore, that you have nothing to do with this 'dark matter' that has been identified as a possible threat to our national security?"

Betty vigorously shook her head and grunted.

"Would it be too much to ask then, madam, if you might demonstrate a...sample of your powers for us here today?" The minister looked sheepishly at Graham as he posed this question. Forsythe nearly fell out of her chair, but Betty seemed to have anticipated the situation.

"We never gives demonstrations on the spur of the moment, Mr. Government Man. It is not our lot to entertain and distract people from the daily dos and don'ts of life, you know?" Betty stared at the three with the assurance of the blessed.

* * *

"Good Lord, man, you didn't!" Avery was anxious to hear everything. "And you actually saw someone that high up in the Ministry of Defence? Well, that's great news. It means that they're taking things seriously." He suddenly went quiet. "What else do you do when the entire country, not to mention the world, is at risk?" He felt quite foolish.

Forsythe took up the slack. "I loved the part where he took for granted that Betty was a witch with special powers and that she had a following and knew how to cast spells. It was right out of an old-fashioned cinema, you know, the kind that—"

"Now, now, Leftenant, that's quite enough." Graham had a hard time controlling himself, as well. "It was a bit comical, I must admit, and when they wouldn't give Betty back her staff, you could smell the cordite burning under her cap." He shook his head in disbelief. "They maintained that there were alien substances on the thing, traces of strange gasses, I think they said."

"Yes. I'm surprised they didn't identify some kryptonite on it as well." Forsythe barely kept from laughing.

Avery managed to sober up. They were at his pub and into their second round, but it wasn't the distilled spirits that were getting to him. "It does appear as though we are getting confirmation of my worst fears, don't you see?" The other two fell silent and pensive. "If Defense is taking this seriously, as it seems they definitely are, we need to try and get whatever information out of Betty that we can. It's obvious that she wouldn't cooperate with government chaps—though you had to try, of course—and yet now she knows that the cat is out of the bag, and that might just work in our favour."

Graham shot a knowing glance at Forsythe at the mention of a cat. Their eyes locked. A frown spread across his features as a thought took hold. "What if we call on Mistress Betty where she is staying with those two fine young ladies...and her cat, Euripides. For some odd reason, I do believe we might make some headway if we can convince the cat to... cooperate."

"Absolutely!" Forsythe was on the same wavelength as her boss. "That cat could be the key to getting at a lot of artifice unsnarled."

Avery couldn't believe his ears. "'Artifice unsnarled?' What the hell does that mean?"

"Simply that, Professor." She began to quiver with excitement. "That damned cat seems to be a major component in Betty's life—a familiar, as they are called—and I think the inspector is on to something. If we can just interrogate that cat..." She blanched at the sound of those last words.

Avery looked from one of his guests to the other in sheer disbelief. He peered into his mug and wondered aloud if the alcoholic content hadn't been diddled with. "I know about familiars, of course, but how do you propose to interrogate a cat? Even one like Euripides?"

"Carefully, old boy. Most carefully." Graham took a long drag on his ale. "Sandy is right, after all. The cat is as meaningful to Betty as her staff, and I have this crazy notion that we can learn a lot if we know how to ask the right questions." He shook his head. "I know that I am not a cat person. It took Sandy to let me know that. But I do know that when that cat was in my home, unbeknownst to me, there were vibrations, energy flows…whatever…that had me giddy *and* lit my pipe."

Forsythe nodded enthusiastically, making Avery even more incredulous. "Lit your pipe? Is that a metaphorical expression for something indecent?"

"No, dammit. Quite literally my pipe lit up spontaneously without a match." Graham went from childish enthusiasm to broad chagrin in moments. "Mind you, I had been trying a little experiment, one that Sandy arrived just in time to witness. But nothing happened until that cat showed itself and fled to the front door where Betty stood waiting for it." His hand shot up. "Now there is a puzzle for you. However did she know that Euripides was in my home?"

Avery set his mug down. This was too much to follow, even over coffee.

Sandy tried to explain. "You must understand that the inspector, when a student, wrote a paper on spontaneous combustion and the powers of the mind." Avery threw his hands in the air but didn't roll his eyes. "And while he was experimenting with his pipe, Euripides snuck into the house and hid. And when I came to the door, somehow the pipe had been lit, and the only way, we think, that it could have happened was for the cat to have done it." She shrugged, as though nothing could have been more straightforward.

"All of that somehow sounds strangely romantic," Avery began, still befuddled. "And my mother was a most devoted cat person, so I do get the drift." He scratched at his beard. "I wonder now, all these years later…"

"No. Your mother? You think?" Sandy was both amused and quite touched. She turned to Graham. "My mother, as we are delving into the dregs of our past, always warned me about the Welsh…but never said anything about their being pixilated – visited by the Little People."

"My dear girl, I do believe we are wandering a bit far from the mark, don't you?" Graham attempted an avuncular frown. "Of course the Welsh are pixilated. Everyone knows that."

Avery managed to hold his council. But this time his eyes did a 360. "When you two are quite ready to get down to business, we have a planet to try and preserve."

"Right you are, of course." Graham set his drink down and managed a sheepish frown at Sandy. "First things first, and that means skinning that cat, if we are agreed."

"Oh, a most unfortunate choice of verbs, sir. We are not angling, I should hope, to in any way intimidate the cat, just discover what we might from…observing its reactions to our questions. Am I right?"

"Of course, of course. Bad choice of words. No intimidation, light interrogation, perhaps a bit of catnip if the bloody little bugger cooperates. Nothing out of the ordinary." Graham clasped his hands on the table and sat back with a sigh.

CHAPTER FIFTEEN

Willy came to the door and frowned when he saw who was there. "It's them, Mother. All three of them. What do you want me to do?"

"Let them in, you blithering idiot. Let them in." Betty sat in the lone high-backed chair in the sitting room with Euripides on her lap. "We were expecting you, gents, and even you, miss." She nodded to the available chairs and couch. "Time for a real powwow, as they say out West."

Graham was relieved to see that the staff had been returned and was lying by Betty's chair. "Time indeed, Mistress Betty. Thank you for seeing us without prior notice, though that seems irrelevant to you."

"Most irrelevant, Inspector. Your intentions were crystal clear as soon as you formed them." She pointed briefly at her head. "A very simple trick, if you are versed in them."

The three took their seats and were relieved to see Willy wander off into the kitchen. Their eyes were all on the cat, who followed Willy with a somnolent stare from Betty's lap. "Would it be too much to ask," ventured Graham, "if your staff was returned in good condition?"

"My what?" Betty was concentrating on petting Euripides, which enticed an enormous purring sound. "Oh, my old walking stick. Yes, they finally saw fit to return it today, and it seems to be in good working order." She leaned over and gave it a pat.

All three smiled at that news. Forsythe fidgeted as Avery cleared his throat and tried to get to the point. "We—I think I can speak for a large number of us—are grateful for your appearance before the minister the other day and only wish there had been a greater meeting of minds."

Betty scoffed. "Meeting of minds? With the likes of those blokes? Not going to happen. Ever. Their idea of 'shared intelligence' is four parts their whimsy and nil parts anything else." Forsythe sat back as Betty launched a wad at a spittoon near her feet.

"We know that they are a tight bunch," Avery continued, trying to find acceptable common ground. "And Lord knows they are more curious than certain about what's happening, so they have little to put forth of their own."

Betty continued to stroke Euripides's back as the purring increased in volume, taking on a hollow resonance that seemed to echo around the room. Graham shook his head, as though trying to clear it of some obstruction. Avery began to do the same. Forsythe sneezed and reached for a handkerchief in her handbag. Betty squinted as though controlling an inner urge. Her eyes darted from one of her guests to the next, measuring their reactions. When tears began to shed from all three, she stopped stroking the cat.

"We can begin to talk now. I think we are all on the same wavelength, as it was." Betty held out a hand to Willy, who had just reappeared from the kitchen. "It is safe now, Son, to sit in on our little discussion." Euripides sat and scanned the room from his perch on Betty's lap. His purring had diminished to a barely audible whir. The three guests all sat as though frozen in place, stricken by a shared stroke.

"You have just experienced a whiff of the power that lies behind the essence of our world, gents and miss. It will hold you in its grip for just a little while, so you knows its force and will not struggle when released from it." She watched as each face began to ease out of its sculpted stiffness. Blank expressions gave way to worried furrows, followed by anxious relief. All three quivered with an excitement that could easily be mistaken for sexual arousal.

"Welcome to the real world, yes? The realm of sound from whence the fury comes." Betty cackled and nodded her head as each turned to gaze at her with wide-eyed distraction. "Now you know a portion of our secrets.

The cat is out of the bag, as you say. Or at least this cat is on the prowl and may be the only help you will get in learning what you seek to know."

Graham was the first to find his voice. "What, where…how did this happen?" He raised his hands and flexed them. His relief was shared by the other two, who now could move and feel and share their fright.

"The 'what,' inspector, is sound, the simple magnification of what all stuff is made from." Betty peered at Graham with the restraint of a scholar speaking to a schoolboy. "And the 'where' is what I believe you were seeking, the dark area between worlds that exists to keep the two apart." She cocked her head to see if anyone had caught her meaning. "The 'how' is not important."

"The 'where' is where?" Avery rubbed his head and tried to focus his eyes.

"The place that has drawn your attention. The area that once was our ally, our co-conspirator in magic, our playground for tricks and treachery." Betty suppressed a sneer. "It was to us like your stages, upon which you strut and fret, where we would conspire and deceive."

Forsythe spoke up. "But for me it was like being caught in a wall of ice and fire, surrounded by sounds that kept me warm and safe."

"Count your blessings, then missy. You are more like that other one, the friend of the professor, who is blessed by innocence." Betty waved a hand dismissively.

Graham blinked and suppressed a cough. "I fear it wasn't like that for me at all. Just the opposite, in fact. Fire and ice, yes, but the sounds I heard were shrill and wanted to tear me apart."

Avery nodded. "Yes, it was terrible, bone chilling, empty."

"I believe you have hit upon it, Professor," Betty exclaimed. "'Empty' is what I fear the most. Where there had been substance"—she held out a cupped hand—"there is nothing left for us to work, to mould, to play with any longer. It has gone rogue and left us with a sense of invalidation that echoes hollow and cold."

Avery shook his head in sheer puzzlement. "My dear lady, wherever did you obtain this sudden vocabulary, this means to articulate so clearly the situation?"

Betty scoffed. "I am not just an old crone for public disdain, my good man." Her voice deepened, and her face again took on the shaded tones of a Lincoln or a Shakespearean surrogate. "We have travelled far and long to get here, through many portals and warps of time and place. And the dark matter that you concern yourself with was our highway to what you might call 'the stars.'"

"Which means?" Avery leaned forward.

"Simply that we may no longer be able to protect our land through our ancient ways." Betty glanced up at Willy, who stood by the window, looking out. "And the generations to come, if there be any, will suffer for it. That alone should give your Defence Ministry cause for alarm."

"Which leaves us…?" Graham held out a hand to Forsythe.

"Which leaves you…us…all up the proverbial creek, Inspector." Betty squinted and took on the appearance of an Asian mystic.

Avery grunted. "At least we have reached a point of reference, if also no return. You say that the space—it exists between two worlds, does it?—has become unreliable, unpredictable, useless. Does that mean that it has changed identity, makeup, consistency?"

Betty leaned down and picked up her staff. "In a word, yes. It has become like one of your computers that breaks down—that 'crashes,' as you say—so that neither the essence nor the former accessibility is there for us now. There are moments, and then there are breakdowns. Nothing is certain."

"But there is also hostility?" Forsythe clung to Graham's hand.

"Most decidedly. But not just hostility." Betty paused to search for the words. "There is, foremost, a sense of revenge, a sense of despair and retribution that would make sense only if the entire universe was made up of atoms that act like children." She shrugged.

"How horrible." Forsythe blanched. "To think that we might all be at the mercy of squabbling brats."

Betty forced a grin and avoided Willy's stare. "Yes, not a fair prospect by any measure."

"I suppose I would be showing my age, Mistress Betty, were I to ask why you told the minister that the dark forces were not part of your world." Graham sat forward and tried to appear nonchalant.

"What I told him was that the force that demolished my home was not of our world, that the threat to his world was not of our world. This was, by then, true. It had taken on the perversity that we have been discussing." She lifted her staff and mumbled an incantation. "Watch now this, for I fear the hour approaches when I can no longer hold back the darkness."

Even as she spoke, a slitting sound assaulted everyone's ears. It was as though a giant tear had rent the essence of existence, creating sound that seemed to come from deepest space—silent and dark but penetrating to the bone. A jagged scar appeared in the middle of the room, stretching from where Betty sat to a point above where Euripides stood arching his back and spitting feline profanities. What appeared to be granules—black, shiny, and weightless—floated out of the slit to drift in sinister forms around the startled group. Even Betty appeared stricken by fear as she tried to dodge a cloud of blackness that gravitated toward her head.

Wielding her staff much like a sword, she cut the cloud in two, crying out in an unknown tongue and levitating out of her chair. The cleft cloud slowly evaporated, and a sweet-scented gas floated in its stead. White as the rest was black, this entity curled in upon itself and soon disappeared. But the rest of the room remained shrouded in darkness, and all but Betty seemed paralyzed by fear.

Finally, making a prodigious leap, Euripides snarled his way through a spiralling cloud and...disappeared. With a cry Betty dropped to her feet and lunged toward the offending cloud. Daring not to assault it with her staff, she reached a bony hand into the blackened space where Euripides had disappeared. Sounding like a beast from a deep jungle, she wrestled with an entity no one else could see. As sweat formed on her brow and desperation deepened the lines on her face, she closed her eyes and seemed to go into a trance.

As the rest watched, Betty now floated along with the cloud that had taken her cat. Half invisible at times, she appeared to have lost consciousness. Willy was the first one to try to save her, to bring her out of whatever influence she had fallen under. It did him no good, pulling as hard as he could and screaming into the dark void that now threatened to claim his mother as well as the cat. It was only when Graham got to his feet and lent a hand that suddenly she popped back into full sight and fell to the floor, exhausted.

Panting and weak, all she could say, over and over again, was "They've got my cat." With an abrupt shift, the black granules and the long slit they had fallen from dissolved. A shrill moan, a deep hum, and then a dull vibration marked the event.

Betty beat her chest, overwhelmed with grief. She kept mumbling in some incoherent fashion as she got to her feet and looked around. The sound of the front door opening and the voices of Fiona and Missy briefly distracted everyone. But Betty's loss was etched on her face, and the two women knew in a flash what must have taken place.

"It's happening." That was all Betty could manage, but it was more than enough, given the appearance of all in the room. "My powers are all but gone, along with my cat." She appeared to shrivel before everyone's eyes. "The force has grown, and we have shrunk accordingly. And now that Euripides is gone…" she just shook her head and fell silent.

Forsythe rubbed her eyes and hoped to come out of what seemed to be a terrible dream. There was one factor that kept pulsating in her skull, that would not dissipate even as she shook her head and tried to rationalize what she had witnessed. She held her right hand up in front of her face and saw that it was vibrating as though she were drunk or having a stroke. Quickly she dropped it to her lap, hoping no one had noticed. But Fiona's sharp eye had caught the move.

"Feeling queasy, dearie?" Fiona put an arm around Forsythe's shoulder, pretending to be sympathetic even as she squeezed her arm out of serious curiosity. "My, you are shivering. That must have been a terrible experience for you." She glanced briefly over at Missy. "The leftenant has suffered a mild case of shock, I do believe. Inspector, perhaps you should take her by a hospital when you have a moment."

"I should think we have all suffered a great deal of shock, young lady." Graham peered closely at his aide and back at Fiona. "If anyone needs to visit a hospital, I dare say it's Mistress Betty here. Though an insane asylum would seem more logical for the rest of us after what I think I saw."

"I can only imagine what must have happened," said Missy in all too casual a manner. She was exchanging thoughts with Fiona telepathically and seemed almost in a trance herself. She put her hands to her head and stood expectantly. With a quiver that shook her whole body, she dropped her hands and seemed to all that she wanted to scream. "There's nowhere to go, nothing even to breathe."

Avery fought the impulse to slap her on the back, even as she turned pale and looked as though she might be sick at any moment. "Careful there. Best to sit, don't you think?" He led her to the couch and motioned to Forsythe to get some water from the kitchen. "Tell us what it feels like, if you can manage."

"Suffocation" was all she could come up with. "My head, it's ringing like a bell was being hammered inside it."

Forsythe quickly added, "That's what I felt, too. Just a loud sound, a deep vibration going off like a siren inside my skull."

Avery took her by the hand and felt the vibrations that were still ringing through her body. "As I feared," he said, turning to Graham. "The elemental makeup of the universe has for some time been postulated as variations on sound." He waved a hand as though to downplay the scholarly spiel. "In short, all solid objects that we know of are comprised of different levels of vibrations. And if our world were to unwind, to unravel, to become inoperable, it would be, some say, by way of sound breaking down and flooding the world as we know it."

Graham grabbed Avery by the shoulders. "What are you saying, man? You mean that we just witnessed the breakdown of the universe?"

"Well, the beginnings of the breakdown, Inspector, at the very least. A preview of what we can expect to happen...everywhere." Avery gripped the other's elbows. "I have no idea how the interaction of dark matter with what we know as our world is being triggered, but we have all just seen what can happen, for whatever reason, right here."

They both looked over at Betty and knew she had been the cause of what they had seen, or at least its perpetrator. Breaking their embrace, they anxiously approached her around the protective stance of Willy. "What can you tell us? What sort of time do we have? What can we do to try and keep this from happening?" Avery pleaded, feeling like a child supplicant at church.

Betty stood and tried to remain calm. She spread her hands in a motion of defeat. "There is a breakdown taking place, as we have foreseen. I cannot define it, beyond knowing that my world has been flooded by foreign material, blocking any means to act against it."

Avery nodded. "Electromagnetic dissonance is what we might call it, for lack of a better expression. It means a basic molecular breakdown is happening, and I believe the cause is not coming from either our sun or any other heavenly body." He squirmed at his use of words.

"Heavenly, you say!" Graham couldn't resist. "How about diabolical instead?"

Avery adjusted his glasses. "As you like, except that it would appear to be a natural phenomenon and thus not really in the realm of religion."

"What? You mean to say what we all just witnessed is a natural consequence of cosmic decay or some such nonsense?" Graham's eyes rolled in disbelief.

Avery looked crestfallen but defiant. "This is what some of us have been trying to alert the world to for ages. It appears to be a basic breakdown in the stasis that has held the world together for millennia." He gestured toward Betty. "Our world, of course. Betty's has acted to keep things in balance all this time, if I am guessing correctly, and her ability to continue to do so is, as you have just heard, gone, or at least it has been badly compromised."

"My dear fellow, are you trying to tell us that all we have known as reality has been preserved and protected by witches, by Betty and her lot?" Graham was aghast but not incredulous.

"So it would seem," Avery admitted. "From what we now know about dark matter, the balance between it and matter and antimatter has been maintained by a singular force that is the province of magic, pure and simple. What some of us call superstition and what many know to be part and parcel of Nature."

Forsythe drew a deep breath, her eyes bulging as she stared from one person to the next. Only Willy turned away, trying to conceal some dark secret. "Are you all totally nuts? Do you expect any of us to believe that the world is unravelling because of a lack of faith in Mother Nature?"

"I don't know!" Avery clenched his fists and stomped a foot loudly on the floor. "I wish to God I did, but that is what my research tells me, for Christ's sake." He stopped, embarrassed by both the outbreak and the profanity.

Betty finally focused her eyes and spat once more. "You have stumbled upon a truth that we have always known, and you scientists could not know for want of humility and proper training." She almost smiled. "It is so difficult for us to share our knowledge, for we must appear as fools in the eyes of your world, where Nature has become an adversary rather than an ally." Her frame seemed to grow again as she straightened up to glare at the three outsiders. "If there is to be hope, then it must exist where artifice cannot thrive, where innocence prevails and simplicity rules."

"My God." Avery turned toward his friends. "I know just what she is talking about."

CHAPTER SIXTEEN

D amien Derwentwater was wrestling with his teakettle when the phone rang. He very nearly didn't answer since the distraction resulted in the spilling of hot water all over the counter of his spacious kitchen. "Blast! Where is Horace when I need him?"

"Your lordship?" The butler appeared from nowhere, buttoning his jacket as he advanced.

"Get the phone, would you? I'm having a bit of difficulty making the simplest staple in the British diet." He shook a singed hand and reached for the butter, which had been destined for a scone and would now serve as a salve for his burn.

"The Derwentwater residence," Horace managed a proper baritone pitch. "Yes, sir. No, sir. He is a bit indisposed at the moment."

"Tell whoever it is that I am in Majorca, would you, Horace?"

"It's a Mr. Owens, sir. He says that it is quite imperative that he speak with you, sir."

"Avery? Well, I suppose I shall have to make a miraculous return from the Mediterranean if he insists on getting through." Damien reached for the phone with his uninjured hand. "What ho, Professor, how may I help you?" A brief glance of thanks to Horace turned quickly to a frozen look of intense concern. "Good Lord, I'll be right round. Your pub? Of course, I do."

The seventh Earl of Derwentwater hung up the phone and winced at the discomfort of his burned hand. "Well, Horace, if you could get me a pub-crawling outfit out—any old tweed will do—I need to see a man about a wi…a woman."

"Very good, sir. An available woman, would it be, sir?"

"Good Lord, no. Betty from Bournemouth is not available in the sense you might have intended, oh devoted man that you are to my best interests." Damien couldn't suppress a grin. "You'll see me married off before my time, or your name isn't Wigglesworth."

"Only thinking of your happiness, sir, lo these many years." A sly look crept across the servant's face.

"Right you are. Marital bliss, with all the trimmings. If I had time to correct your misapprehension of life as it truly is, I would deliver a Sterling Series Lecture on the subject, but as it is, there seems to be a deadline out there that my learned friend thinks I can influence, so I must be off."

"As you say, sir. An older tweed, one for the country, a bit worn and seedy, coming right up."

Damien shook his head as he hailed a cab moments later and tried to brace himself for what appeared to lie ahead. The burn was soon forgotten as he pulled up to the Mole and Hedgehog. Avery was at his usual table, along with Inspector Graham and young Leftenant Forsythe. He was a bit surprised not to see Betty. Introductions were made, and explanations were swift and to the point. Damien listened with an increasing sense of alarm and disbelief.

"Surely there has to be some alternative possibility here, some slightly less-radical—might I say 'bonkers'—cause for your concern."

Forsythe choked on her drink as she hurried to answer. "You just cannot begin to believe what we saw, what we all felt." Her face was flush with excitement and agitation. "It was the sounds that I remember most, the strange silence that was so loud and the many ranges of vibration."

Damien took a closer look at this young lady, who seemed so collected even as she was all but shaking with disbelief. "You say that the silence was loud? How does that work?" He ordered a pint and sat back in his chair, fully aware of the tension that existed around the table.

"If I could explain it, I would expect a Nobel Prize in physics," Avery jumped in. "Sandy is right. For all the darkness and disappearance of the cat, the lasting impression for me, too, was the sound, the penetrating sense of power that came from a ringing or trembling entity that had complete control of the room—not just us, but everything in it, furniture and books as much as any living thing."

"And Betty was all but taken by this thing, swallowed up and treated like a rag doll?" Damien was incredulous.

Avery lifted a hand toward the inspector. "If it hadn't been for Graham here, she might well have wound up wherever her cat went. That was something to behold. Poor Betty floating around in a trance, it looked like, half swallowed by this monstrous cloud until Willy and the inspector managed to yank her away from its grip. Bloody marvellous!"

"Bloody scary, it all sounds to me." Damien reached for his newly delivered drink and lifted it tentatively. "Wish I could say 'cheers' and all that." He cast an appreciative eye around the table. "At least I can say, 'Well met' in spite of the timing."

Graham spoke up, noticing the inordinate time Damien was spending sizing up Forsythe. "We were told, sir, that you might hold a clue to what is transpiring or at least have some knowledge of what we might plan on."

"Me? Good Lord. Who could have told you that?" Damien was taken totally by surprise.

"None other than Betty herself," Avery answered, pulling his chair in close. "You remember when she took your measure and proclaimed you— what was it she said?—an 'innocent.' Someone who could understand the harmonies of nature better than the rest of us."

"But that was just because I brought up the Bushmen of the Kalahari, surely. We all revere what they stand for, after all."

Graham stirred uncomfortably in his seat. "I'm not sure I'm quite on the same page here. What is the relevance of a bunch of Hottentots to our predicament?"

"Oh, Inspector," Forsythe interjected, "how can you say that?" She tried to hide her embarrassment unsuccessfully. "The Bushmen of Southern Africa are among the most sensitive beings on two feet on the planet."

"I stand corrected, Leftenant. Thank you for your vehemence." Graham remained uncomfortable as he looked helplessly from Sandy to Damien and then to Avery. "My old-world background would appear to be catching up with me, I fear."

"Never worry, Inspector," Avery countered. "Your Scottish heritage will kick in at any moment and prove to keep you in tune with our needs."

"I'm so glad you brought up needs," Damien ventured. "Just what do you envision there is for me to do?"

"Well, old chap, I was thinking that Betty probably had something along the lines of the vestal virgins for you." Avery kept as straight a face as he could manage.

Forsythe chimed in quickly. "Ah, yes, the slaughter of the innocents, perhaps. Certainly a prime offering on the altar of expediency." She put a delicate hand over her mouth to conceal the merriment creeping forth. "A quick trip up to Stonehenge might just work wonders."

Avery and Graham both looked shocked at this outburst of levity. Avery was the first to react. "My dear young lady...you might just have an excellent idea there."

Forsythe shook her head. "I am so sorry. I don't know what made me say that. I am so embarrassed."

All four suddenly stiffened with recognition of what Forsythe had said. "Stonehenge." They all fell quiet, and the three looked closely at Damien.

He looked back like a mouse in a lab. "That's not very amusing, you know." He avoided looking at Sandy as he knew she was blushing crimson. Then it struck him, too. "I suppose there could be something in a visit to those stones. I've always had the greatest fascination with the place, after all. Spent the night there once. Nothing happened." He shrugged. "Very disappointing."

Graham tried to right his ship. "Well, this time we might be a bit more fortunate. I mean, we might have some real insight into...the mysteries." He threw up his hands.

"I do think it is worth a try," said Avery. "You never can tell...and we all know that there is something magical about the place, whatever our backgrounds."

"And whatever our beliefs." Damien lifted his mug. "To the mysteries and to unravelling them in time to save us all."

* * *

131

Betty complained most of the way out the M3 motorway until they set off on the quiet back roads of the Wiltshire countryside. Damien was at the wheel of his Range Rover, feeling both excited and most uncomfortable. The sun was setting and caused frequent discomfort by blazing into everyone's eyes. But the moment was dawning, everyone felt, for a possible insight into the full range of danger they might be facing. Betty quickly squelched uneasy joking about the possible prehistoric uses of Stonehenge and admonished all to respect their elders.

"Are you implying, Mistress Betty," Avery had to ask, "that we are all descendants of the creators of that mythic circle of stone?"

Betty pulled reflectively on her chin for a moment before answering. "I cannot swear that your every drop of blood is drawn from their pool, Master Scientist, but The Builders, as we know them, left many lines of intermarriage with the locals. It was their plan to populate the land with useful offspring." She grunted. "Even they could make mistakes."

Forsythe piped up. "I've heard that story—that ancient travellers from outer space came here to interbreed for devilish purposes."

"Not devilish, miss. Just selfish, if you will." Betty scanned the passing countryside now for what had to be landmarks that spoke to her.

"Well, Betty, are you a direct descendant? Is that what makes you more sensitive to nature than the rest of us?" Graham leaned forward with the hope of impressing his aide.

Betty paused. "My heritage is beyond the dating of The Builders." She let that sink in for a moment. "My own story can be traced, you might say, to the stars themselves."

Avery paid particular notice to this statement, knowing the popular theory that all living things were composed of stardust. He felt certain this woman was speaking more than metaphorically or even literally. Something remained unclear, however. "But Betty, if the Builders were from the stars, from far away, how does that make you different?"

"It is not important." She grew ever more excited as they entered the broad expanse of the Salisbury Plain, at the heart of which lay their destination. "My beginnings are of no greater consequence than those of any living thing." The words drifted from her as though once more from a trance.

Graham picked up on the pronouncement. "That has the ring of something I should be able to remember from the Bible. God cares for even the least of his creations, something about sparrows, I believe."

Everyone gave this a moment's thought. "Surely you're not suggesting that Betty is quoting chapter and verse of Christian doctrine, as we approach one of the great symbols of pre-Christian beliefs." Avery spoke for the lot. All eyes concentrated on the inspector.

"Not exactly, no. Of course not, and I am poorly qualified to speak of such things at any rate. But"—he held up a hand defensively—"there is an echo, at any rate, of what I remember from my school days in what Betty just said."

The outline of the famous giant circle of stone broke the horizon, even as the sun began its descent below the edge of the world and a tour bus pulled out of the parking lot. Everyone's attention turned to the stark, silent sentinels of an ancient people who had managed to breach the millennia through methods that would challenge modern means.

Sandy Forsythe put a hand on Damien's shoulder as they pulled into the shadows of the circle. The tension she felt was immediate and palpable.

The inspector eventually persuaded a national parks attendant that their mission should allow then access to the circle after hours, and they proceeded onto the grounds of the monument as dusk threw its mantle of deception over the scene. Flashlights were distributed for when true darkness fell, and the small group made its way to the centre of the circle, led by Betty, who continued to seem to be in a trancelike state. Her head would swing from left to right like a mechanical scanner. Emotion was absent, even as her body began to obtain weightlessness. Her feet barely brushed the worn grass where the group found themselves.

It seemed like hours that they stood, being scrutinized by the mystical collection of inscrutable stones. Sandy was the first to comment on the feeling that emanated from all around them. Looking closely at Damien, she murmured her thought. "Do you feel it?" She turned full circle, taking in the array of the massive dilapidated expression of power that surrounded them. "Do you feel the intensity of emotion that I am getting?"

Damien didn't dare to look at her. His head was much like Betty's, scanning back and forth like a robot's. The last rays of sunlight illumined his face, and Sandy could see that his eyes were darting from stone to stone, as though seeking clues. There was fear in his expression, but determination fought for dominance.

Graham and Avery stopped their inspection of nearby fallen blocks and concentrated their attention on Damien now as he began to wander from one prehistoric slab to another. Betty, too, stopped her seemingly aimless meander and settled on a perch to watch the proceedings.

A sudden absence of light occurred as the sun fully set. The impact on everyone was immediate and gripping. It was as though a giant door had been slammed shut, and there was no escape from whatever force had suddenly appeared. Avery and Graham exchanged glances as Forsythe gasped and reached to take Damien's arm. Even Betty showed a startled recognition of something dire. Everyone fell into a state of suspended animation, of suspenseful anticipation. The darkness was oddly palpable, thick with dread and threat and even the smell of temper.

Betty made an attempt to raise her staff but sat frozen and barely able to let out a whimper. Damien stood as though struck by a long-shadowing spear from *The Iliad*. His torso bent forward, shoulders stooped, and head bowed. His knees began to buckle, but at the sound of Sandy's outcry, they slowly straightened as though bearing some tremendous weight. A sudden silence engulfed the scene, a silence so extreme that the call of a nearby whippoorwill was stilled, as was all else. The little group stood transfixed, unable to move, barely able to breathe.

Avery fought the hardest to overcome the sense of futility they all felt in trying to combat the oppressive weight of darkness. He had foreseen the possibility of just such a tidal force. He knew that the vacuum caused by cosmic dissonance, multiplied by the ancient expressions of pride and premonition, were bound to create the perfect storm of despair. He could feel his blood run cold as he managed to lift an arm to help prop Damien up as invisible forces buffeted him as if determined to test his every fibre. The innocent was thrust into the maelstrom of demonic forces that seemed to delight in letting loose millennia of anger and retribution.

Damien now stood, or rather stooped, in what appeared to be a vortex of angry bees. The support he was getting from Sandy and Avery seemed his only link with the world around him, which was now gathering its will to destroy him. A horrible sound suddenly rent the stillness. The reverberations all could feel emanating from the standing prophets of the past penetrated to the bone. Eyes watered, heads reeled, and barely a breath was taken. For longer than even Betty could calculate, the searing sounds of screaming spirits tore through the little group, with Damien at the epicentre, frozen as a pillar of salt, bent and helpless.

They all heard a distinct cry of anger and defeat, which rose to a shrill climax of quivering rage. Slowly the darkness gave way to the soft tones of dusk, and the oppressive weight of the emotions that had assaulted the group lifted. The sounds of the whippoorwill floated across the tattered landscape, and all could breathe again. Damien slowly straightened his battered body and let out a sigh that echoed mysteriously around the stones.

"Do you think it's over? Was that just the beginning?" Sandy was all but overwhelmed by the experience and could barely stand to embrace the exhausted Damien.

"If that was just the beginning, I want a second opinion about the whole idea." Damien threw a grateful arm around Sandy's shoulders as he worked his way over to sit by Betty. "How do you read all this, Mistress Betty? Did I pass or fail? Is there hope?"

"My dear young man, you have given us all a lesson in pure grit, you have." She looked for an appropriate spot to spit. Finding none and remembering where she was, she refrained. "Whether it's Horatio at the bridge or Lord Nelson at Trafalgar, you can takes your pick. You're among history's champs, you are."

"Why, thank you, ma'am. I suspect Horatio, the elder, would be more to my liking, as his lordship did not survive that fateful battle off the Spanish Main. But what can you make of what we just experienced? And is Sandy right—that that was just the first round?"

Betty took a long time to consider both the question and the young lady who gazed at her now with a bold look of enquiry. "I'm thinking that we have seen all we are about to see here." She paused. "Though I wouldn't have believed a thing had I not seen it with my own eyes and heard it with me ears." She poked a finger in one ear and winced. "That was the most noise I've heard from that sector since Methuselah was a boy." Finally coming to the point, she asked, "How did they treat you, Son?"

Damien sat and extended his arms, glad to see he still had both hands attached that he could flex. "I don't know that I have the words to describe it. You say 'they' as though it were a group, and all I can say is that it did seem like a gang of thugs was battering me, hooligans taunting me. But for all the bombast, there was a sense of a protective power that warded off the worst of it."

Betty nodded and took a closer look at Sandy. "Yes, you were well protected, it would seem, not only by your…background but by more immediate factors." She smiled and made an effort to stand. "I think we have learned a great deal from your little encounter with the spirits of this place. They are angry, of course, but they are unable to act with the destruction they would like, the force that they yet need to settle old scores."

"Whatever do you mean by that?" Sandy was beside herself with curiosity.

Betty squinted, trying to hide the pain she felt. "Why, the torment that you have visited upon the land, the earth, the womb from whence you have sprung." She drew a deep breath and once again appeared to grow several inches in stature. "Don't you know what those spirits were? Why they are so angry?"

Avery interjected. "As I feared, you are saying they are the manifestation of the planet's soul, the angry gods of the land, the trees, and rivers?"

Betty raised a hand and looked all but regal. "That is the purpose of this place, to concentrate the power of those 'gods,' as you put it." She shrugged as she paused to caress a fallen giant as they passed out of the ring and headed back to the artificial light of the parking lot.

"But what have we learned? What can you tell us about what to expect?" Graham trailed Betty like a courtier his queen.

"All I know is that the spirits were unable to do harm to your friend, as I suspected." She cast a brief look toward Damien that betrayed both confidence and relief. "That only means that there may yet be time before… the piper must be paid."

A collective groan went up. Avery opened the door for Betty to take the front seat opposite Damien as the rest piled onto the opposing benches in the back. The darkness that lay just at the edge of the parking lot had the look of a crouching animal, waiting to pounce.

CHAPTER SEVENTEEN

Missy and Fiona had had enough of Willy's moodiness since Euripides's disappearance. He seemed inconsolable, complaining that nothing in his life ever worked out, ever brought him a moment of happiness. Until, that is, that brief time when the cat had chosen to sit on his lap so shortly before disappearing. All three, however, were anxious to hear what might have happened at Stonehenge, so when the doorbell rang, there was a swift shared response.

Willy managed to get to the door first. "Well, Mother, what say you? What happened to all those disbelievers when the darkness fell?" He stepped back as Betty entered, spluttering and impatient.

"You should have seen the chaos. All Hell broke loose." She nodded, savouring the expression then sat down with a grateful sigh. "That old pile of stones really can conjure up a good show still. Not quite like the good old days but better than sittin' at home." She cackled quietly to herself.

"But what was the take?" Fiona was the most agitated. "What can we expect from the results? What did the mortals do to survive?"

"Now, now. One question at a time." Betty looked quite petulant. "The 'take,' as you calls it, is that we are just where I feared. Cut off. Without Euripides, even with my staff, I was powerless. The only force working out there was innocence, pure and simple." She smacked her lips at that witticism. "That Damien boy is as pure as the driven snow, and he has a girlfriend, whether he knows it or not, that reinforced his power to resist the forces of temptation."

"So, where does that leave us?" Missy mirrored Fiona's agitation.

Betty spat. "As I said, cut off, powerless, overwhelmed."

The three looked at each other with a growing sense of helplessness. Only Willy gave voice to their shared thoughts. "But, Ma, that means we all go down with the ship, right? Without Euripides, and with everything so stirred up, what hope have we?"

"Precious little, Son. Precious little." Betty scratched at her scalp for a pensive moment. "Unless we can latch onto the shield that the young feller carries and make some leap of faith to get back my cat…"

"That would be great, huh, Mother? To get Euripides back would be like…catching a rainbow."

Betty turned to scowl at her son. "What you been drinkin', Son? 'Catching a rainbow'? Are you out of your scrawny mind?"

"Now, Betty, don't be so hard on your son like that." Fiona surprised herself by wrapping a protective arm around Willy's shoulders. "If he is going to wax poetic about your cat, you should be happy."

Betty barely heard this plea. She kept repeating the word *rainbow*, frowning, and looking around the room. "Now where did I put that cursed pot?"

Willy's eyes widened. "You mean that western piece of clay? That thing from some pueblo in New Mexico that you would never let me near?"

Betty shot a look of annoyance at her son. "Yes, you pathetic…you poor benighted soul, deprived all these years from playing with what may be our last hope to find Euripides." She continued to scan the room with increasing annoyance.

"You mean that beautiful black pot with the special markings?" Fiona sat up and tried to look innocent.

"Yes" came the immediate reply as Betty sprang to her feet. "What have you done with it? I don't see it anywhere."

"Why, it was so mysteriously beautiful, I put it in my bedroom. I didn't think you'd mind…"

"Mind? Me, a simple servant of the forces of light and darkness? Mind?" Betty nearly rose off the floor without the help of her staff. "I'm sure you wouldn't mind if I borrowed your spleen for a short trip to Mars or excavated your heart from that miserable excuse of a chest?" Her eyes sent off sparks even as they darkened to the density of coal.

Fiona was through the door to her bedroom before Betty had finished her diatribe and returned with the object in question clutched to her bosom. Her expression was of sheer pain and penance. "I had no idea that it had such importance for you. I'm so sorry I ever touched it."

Betty let out a sigh of relief as she reached out for her magic talisman and even nodded by way of thanks and apology for her outburst. "You were not supposed to know. Not even my son was to know." She held the polished black piece of art, as solid yet sublime as a sculpture, and cradled it as though it were a child. "This is my only other means to conjure up the force needed to counter what is happening all around us. My staff proved all but worthless at the stones, and with my cat gone from me to the other side, I am but helpless were I to lose this...channel to my ancestors."

"You mean you have Injun blood, Ma? Which means I have some too, right?" Willy all but danced with joy.

"Of course, you have Indian blood, boy, but not in the way you think." Betty scowled. "It's a lot more thinned out over the years and generations and such." She gestured at Fiona and Missy. "These two have some, too. We all do, along with the African, Asian, and whatnot. What did you learn at school, anyway? Nothing beyond Hadrian's Wall? Nothing that doesn't wear a kilt and raise Cane with those blessed pipes?"

Willy winced. "Not much, I guess, except to be your apprentice and try to keep my yap shut."

Betty relented. "Well, you have done a good job of pretending to be as dumb as a post, Son, I'll give you that." She set the pot down on the small but sturdy dining table and went about stalking the flat for a variety of artefacts. Seashells materialized from the bookshelves. Dried flowers were plucked from their vases around the room. Fruit from the kitchen and a handful of kitty litter rounded out the collection of improbable objects scattered around the base of the pueblo Indian creation.

Paying no attention to the others in the room, Betty began to murmur words that soon took wing and echoed around the small flat with the persistence of a beating heart. The three observers fell silent and soon were caught up in the rhythmic chanting that seemed to emanate not only from Betty but equally from every corner of the room. Betty's stooped figure floated by the table's edge, moving in measured steps, as though dancing around a primitive fire that gave her both warmth and a light to see into another world.

Slowly her pace increased, and her body seemed ever more a part of the ether. The chanting rose and fell in volume. Willy was particularly taken by the scene. His mother was acting just like the Native Americans he had seen in movies, swept up in sound and movement, uncaring about any manifestation of the world around her. The ritual went on for what seemed like hours, though the sun outside didn't set and time, and temperament receded into an insignificant corner.

Gradually Betty slowed her deliberations, always concentrating on the gleaming pot, even touching it with a tentative hand from time to time, as though beseeching it to grant her wishes.

Eventually she stopped. Obviously exhausted, she retreated to the couch where she sat with a loud, piercing wail of defeat. "They won't give me back my Euripides. The thieving…the soulless brigands have him ready to be dispatched beyond the stars, far beyond my memories or control, even though it is not our kind that has set them into such a rage."

Willy looked particularly puzzled. "But that would mean that they have adopted the ways of the mortal world. If they have started to be as wilful and bitchy as that, there is surely no hope."

"That's precisely what I have been saying lo these past many days, boy." Betty managed to withhold a further withering comment on her son's intellect. "We have the basic problem of being abandoned by our spirit world, *not* for anything we have done…unless they consider us responsible for keeping matters right, which is what we have done lo these past many centuries." She suddenly sat up. "Damnation! That is what's at the bottom of this, I'll warrant."

Missy groaned. "You mean that the behaviour of bankers and politicians and other scurrilous lots is now our responsibility?" She blanched. "What a horror to think."

Fiona frowned. "I think what dear Betty is saying, and I guess she is right about this, is that we are the keepers of the flame, the wardens of propriety, the overseers of balance in this world, and we have failed as much as anyone."

"Poppycock!" Missy was at first totally offended but slowly saw the logic in what had just been said. "Dammit, that's just not fair. We try to lead a quiet life of subtle interaction with our mortal neighbours, and if they get out of hand, we get the blame. That's a buggering lot of bilge water."

"Well said, my dear." Betty nodded approvingly. "But as well as you put it, the bottom line is that we are all up against the judgment of history and not our peers, as they says in the movies."

A strained silence fell on the room. Anger and puzzlement etched each face, even Willy's. "Why don't you just tell these forces to bugger off, Mother?" His tone hinted at a churlish whine.

Betty rolled her eyes and fumed to herself, managing only to flex her fingers like her cinematic equivalent in *The Wizard of Oz*. Another instance of aggravation would surely cause smoke to spout from her ears. Willy wanted to see that. Before he could speak again, she leapt to her feet.

"That's it, boy. You may well have hit the spike on the noggin!" She cast a cryptic eye at the two women watching her with anxious looks and winked. "Bugger off, it will be if I can just manage to remember a certain incantation from years gone by."

Willy's face lit up. If there was one thing that his mother did that actually made him proud, it was getting her dander up and testing the patience of the universe. A lopsided grin formed as his eyes darted back and forth between his mother and Missy and Fiona. A sleeve swept across his mouth to contain the saliva that began to flow in anticipation of major fireworks.

"They think they have me over a barrel, do they?" Betty seemed to fold herself into a ball, twisted and bent over and ready to be hurled through space at some unsuspecting target of the mind. Willy was as wound up as any witness to a medieval execution might be, lusting for blood and the most basic stroke of justice. The others held their breath and couldn't avert their eyes from the ball of fury that began to pulsate under the smouldering garment that was Betty's cloak.

Low moans gave way to louder intermittent shrieks, punctuated by babblings of ancient tongues and obvious defiance. Sparks formed above Betty's head, and all three onlookers shrank away from the core of the reaction, which increasingly resembled a mad experiment gone haywire. Even Willy's wild-eyed enthusiasm turned to sweat-soaked fear as the air above his mother turned green and incandescent and ugly.

A flash of light and the impact of sound that split the very atoms in the air hurled everyone to his or her knees. Tears of blood seeped from every eye. Consciousness became a fleeting illusion. Pain and blindness held total sway in the tiny space that enclosed the lot. Fury was all encompassing, Then came utter, total silence, except a pulsating sound that seemed to come from the breathing of some malevolent being that had swallowed the room and all its inhabitants.

Wiping her eyes, Betty took a tentative look around. Dazed and in obvious pain, she nonetheless nodded in uncertain hope. "If that doesn't give us a fightin' chance, I don't know what might."

"What did you tell 'em, Mother? Did you threaten 'em with...?" Willy paused and went blank. "What the hell could you threaten 'em with, huh?"

"You're getting brighter by the moment, boy. Hell is as close as anything that I...brought up as a possibility of a threat. Not that that would make any difference to the powers what be, mind you."

"Whatever it was, it sure got a reaction." Missy cleared her face and worked on her ears for several moments.

"It seemed as though we were in the middle of a storm cloud, Betty." Fiona fumbled for words. "What happened? Who did you enlist?"

Betty allowed herself a slight smile of self-indulgence. "Good guess. It was that addle-pated son of mine that gave me the idea. He does deserve some credit here." She gathered herself and managed to unwind back into a semblance of verticality. "We witches of Britain, as proud of our heritage as we are and always should be, are not the only wielders of special powers." She brushed off the front of her skirt with a decisive gesture. "While it pains me some, there are plenty of other players on the field, as it were. The shamans of the Americas are legion, after all, and the Old People all over the globe still have much magic, even though only a shadow of their former strength. It is they who may have some influence over the Dark Ones, and it is they whom I tried to enlist in our fight for survival here."

"What chance do you think we have now?" Missy seemed unimpressed. "What difference can anyone make now, with the odds so much against us?"

Betty took only brief notice of this defeatist attitude. She winced from the pain of probability and quickly dismissed the thought of defeat. "The Dark Ones are in no mood to reason. They only now want to destroy all that humans have brought upon themselves, the glitter and greed and meanness. What I have just done is to try and enlist all the white witches and shamans and medicine men of the world to make a stand, to pool our strengths to combat the threat that the Dark Force is trying to destroy us with."

"But, Mother, if you couldn't get Euripides back using that black pot there on the table, how do you think you can succeed at…anything twice as hard?" Willy's eyes darted with a mixture of doubt and sadness between his mother's bent form and the gleaming black example of Native American craftsmanship.

"If this were as hard as your head, Son, I'd have to agree with you. It would be impossible. But by the grace of Zeus, there is still a chance that our kind can survive." Betty swivelled her head to spit. "The only hope I see is that we are burdened with bringing along the rest of the world that isn't worth a bucket of spit." She stopped suddenly and lifted a weak hand to her head. "And the only hope for the whole bunch of us is through the intercession by…the crippled of mind." She shook her head as though she had just relayed words that made no sense to her.

"'The crippled of mind'? What on earth does that mean?" Fiona nearly fell over from exhaustion and wonder.

"One thing is for certain," Betty said. "It does not mean, my son, as crippled between the ears as he may be." She frowned and tried to decipher the expression. "Crippled." She squinted and grunted and squirmed. As her right hand rose in a dismissive sweep before her face, she turned with a look of triumph to the others. "Of course. Those who have undeveloped psyches, naturally shrivelled egos, unfed ambitions, pools of self-lessness—saints, innocents, *idiots*!" She cackled so loudly that her listeners' skin crawled. "I should have known! We need to find that lad from the stones!"

CHAPTER EIGHTEEN

Damien Derwentwater felt a decided chill run up his spine. He made a quick search for open windows and reluctantly realized it wasn't a draft that had caught him unawares. The sound of his doorbell ringing insistently reinforced the premonition that not only was there cause for alarm but whatever it was had him in its sights. He barely managed to peer down at the huddled lot below before he wished he had followed his instinct to head up to the country for the weekend.

"Nothing ventured, nothing gained" coursed through his mind, quite uninvited, as he nimbly descended the stairs to let the visitors in. "Well, what a surprise!" was all he could manage as the three ladies and Willy all tumbled into the marble-floored foyer. Betty gave him an unusually queer look but was otherwise trying to control herself and kept quiet as Missy spoke for the lot.

"We are so glad that you are here, Damien." She seemed all but apoplectic with relief. "We were afraid that you might have retreated up-country after our visit to Stonehenge...the wilderness and all, you know."

"Wilderness?" Damien all but burst out laughing. "You mean those bloody awful demons trying to tear me apart? A bit more than wilderness, that, if you ask me."

"Of course. You know what I mean." Missy threw up her hands in frustration.

Betty looked in vain for a spittoon. "We are so grateful, your lordship, that you would go along with our little experiment there amongst the stones." She shot an angry look at Missy and stepped close to Damien. "It was all powerful brave of you to stand up to those…spirits what overtook us all there in the fateful ring." She plastered a smile on her pasty face and drew a deep breath. "We were all so impressed by your strength to resist the forces of temptation—I believe that was what was happenin'—and not turn a hair greyer."

Even Willy groaned at this pretence, and Damien just braced for whatever was to come. "I suspect you have a follow-up test for me, have you, Mistress Betty? A friendly broomstick to ride? Orcs to slay? Hmm?"

"I wish it were that simple, I really do." Betty thought she might have a lead-in. "Is there a chance we can discuss the matter in the privacy of your quarters, your lordship?" She scanned the hallway as though it might be crawling with unwanted souls.

"By all means." Damien caught himself checking for suspicious shadows before quickly ushering everyone up the broad flight of stairs to his study.

"The servants all tucked in their beds, are they?" Betty wrung her hands and tried in vain to seem composed.

Damien's eyebrows rose a notch. "My one manservant, Horace, is off for the weekend—fishing, I do believe, the lucky bugger."

Betty nodded, frowning at the prospect of someone actually enjoying themselves at such a time. "Well, it can't be helped."

"I beg your pardon?" Damien quickly decided to let that comment go as he braced for the broadside of requests he was certain were imminent. "Do you mind if I give a call to my friend, Avery Owens? I suspect he might be interested in what you have to say." His hand was on his old-fashioned phone before there was any chance of a response. Moments later he was in the kitchen, preparing tea for the lot. Avery would be around by the time he had everything settled.

"What we was hopin' you might help us with, your lordship," Betty began tentatively, "was to accompany us to our little pub and help us get the pulse of a very difficult situation we might be experiencin'."

Damien squinted at this thought as though it were the first light of the last dawn of eternity. "Sounds serious, Mistress Betty. If it's that mysterious pub of yours you want me to visit, I am definitely going to want the company of my friend, Avery. He should be here any moment."

Betty made silent contact with her three companions, then nodded her agreement. "He will be made welcome, sir, as a special token of our gratitude to you."

The doorbell sounded, and Damien jumped to his feet. "There we are. You all finish your tea. I'll be right back up." Hurrying down the stairs, he opened the door with a sudden sense of fear he had never known before. "My dear fellow. Well met. Come in. My apologies for the hour and the urgency. We have the honour of Betty of Bournemouth with her retinue upstairs in quite a tizzy, it would seem, wanting me to go with them to that mysterious pub of theirs."

Avery's eyes widened, then shrank to slits. "Good Lord, man. Things are that bad, are they?"

"So it would seem, dear chap. I have them swilling tea for the moment, but I know it's going to take more than caffeine to clear this little matter up. Are you with me?"

"To the last drop of whatever they conjure up at the pub, dear fellow. I feel less than ready for full frontal combat than I once did, but a pint or two of bitter should be no great shock to my system."

As they climbed the stairs, Betty stood at the top, more than ready to head out. "We thanks you for the tea, Damien—may I call you that?—but time is of the essence now, we are quite sure, and if we can just go 'round to our little publick house, we can better understand what we have to deal with, if you get my meaning."

With a minimal amount of grumbling and several odd turns through the darkened streets of town, the group arrived, as if by magic, at the well-lit establishment known as the Goat and Dragon.

A glum crowd was gathered inside, and all eyes followed the newcomers as they made their way to a back table near the bar. Betty propped her staff in a corner and gave a stern nod to the bartender, who was already busy preparing them all drinks.

"May I suggest a special concoction for the occasion, gentlemen?" Betty tried to hide her anxiety with little effect. "It's an old family recipe, as they say, one that should take the edge off the night and add an edge to the cause." She suppressed a smile as best she could. "We all need a little edge now and then."

"I was looking forward to a pint myself," Avery ventured but gave in to the withering look he caught. "Whatever floats our collective boat, I suspect, is what we should be thinking."

"Precisely, my dear professor." Betty gave a sharp kick to Fiona under the table as she was about to say something. "We have come to the point—lamentable as it may be—where we must try and cooperate, to act together, or we shall surely perish together."

"'Perish,' did you say?" Avery felt his face flush and seem to melt around the edges.

Silence in the room was broken only by the efforts of the bartender to complete his task. Hoisting his tray with a grunt, he shuffled the short distance to the table and silently circled the group, setting down an odd reddish-brown substance in old-fashioned pewter mugs that appeared to give off steam, though the drinks weren't hot.

Damien and Avery just stared at their offerings, unable to do more than wrap their hands around the worn metal relics of an earlier age. The level of anxiety around the table was palpable, though Betty tried to break the spell by raising her mug and pronouncing some incomprehensible notion.

"Your linguistic skills are most enviable, may I venture." Avery bowed as he acknowledged what all were thinking. "May I ask what dialect, what exact language, that was you were using?"

Betty seemed quite startled at such a question. She paused for a moment, then slid a slender hand across the table toward where Avery sat. "That was just a few words from the edge of nowhere, my dear professor, a long-lost dialect that some people say had its origins…far away." Her eyes briefly lifted skyward.

Damien felt an odd sense of calm at hearing the words of this strange tongue. He was about to say something when Missy interrupted. "I don't believe I've ever heard you identify that language you sometimes lapse into, Betty. Are you going to let us all know more about it?"

Betty frowned and sank into what seemed to be a state of suspended animation. She sat there for several moments, all eyes from around the room now turned on her. Slowly, a twitch stirred the right side of her face, and she began to come back from wherever it had been that called her. She muttered something about frequencies, shook her head, and stared glumly around the table. "There is little hope, I fear. The response from around the world does not amount to a shadow of the energy that we need to deal with the Dark Ones."

Damien stirred once more, this time uninterrupted. "Are these Dark Ones you speak of the same as the spirits I encountered at Stonehenge?"

Betty's face twitched noticeably. "In a manner of speaking, yes." She hesitated. "They are not true 'ones,' if you catch my meaning. They are more a collection of energy that I find easier to deal with, when I am able, to think of as spirits, divisible and somehow separate, rather than just the great collection of emotion that has now taken the form of total hostility to...man."

"And by 'man,' you mean all of us here, for example," Damien ventured, feeling increasingly under a strange spell as he finally raised his drink and took a tentative sip.

Avery and the others watched with an all-but-morbid fascination, then followed suit, tasting their drinks with deep uncertainty that gave way to relief that bordered on euphoria. "Whatever is in this stuff?" Avery wondered half aloud.

"An ancient brew," Betty murmured. "Old family recipe, as I told you." Her head swivelled around to confront the room at large. "Give us your blessings, my pretties, for what we undertake today. This even may be the last chance we have to save our souls." She waved her right hand well above her head in a gesture of faith that brought a low humming sound from all in the room. Then she turned her attention to Damien and gently laid a hand on his. "We must initiate you into the ring of energy, from whence you may have the strength to help us all escape the wrath of the Dark Ones."

Damien just nodded, even as Avery caught his breath and felt his whole body shaking from the sudden sense of dread that settled low over the table. The phrase "nothing ventured, nothing gained" coursed through Damien's mind once more, unbidden. Somehow, the sense of forboding wasn't as disturbing as it ought to have been, from all he could imagine. The energy he began to pick up from being there, surrounded by Betty's cohorts, sent a tingling sensation up his spine, where it burrowed into a part of his brain that he had never been aware of before. Deep pulsations from an inner realm of primitive impulses all but turned him to stone. At least, that was how he felt. Petrified in a manner that went far beyond fear. In fact, he felt a sudden flash of understanding of the ancient Japanese warrior concept of thinking beyond death, in order not to fear it. He had somehow skirted the immediate prospect of dying, of being crushed beneath an avalanche of anger and retribution by the spirit world, and sat afloat in a sea of grim determination, not calm but composed.

All eyes were now on him, especially Betty's, whose dark pupils seemed to pulsate with the same frequency that now came from his core. Images formed, dim and shimmering at first, that served to seduce his mind into a raw sense of purpose, of resolve, of a state of mind that clamoured for precision beyond anything he had managed to avoid in his privileged life. He lifted his mug once more, uncertain, but now needy.

The others at the table sat in steely silence, even Avery, who knew more than he wanted to about the ordeal that was taking shape. As one they all now drank deeply of the potion Betty had ordered. A haze appeared to hover over the table as their breath came in short bursts of steam.

Damien could just manage to keep his mind focused on the others at the table, his eyes now slits of pain that couldn't conceal his fear. He had no idea what it was that threatened him and all he knew, except the memory of his being assaulted at Stonehenge. A rehearsal for this engagement, he dimly realized. But where were the angry furies? They seemed to be circling like a pack of wolves or sharks or whatever might be worse. He felt a certain security somehow, sitting there, as yet unassailable, though far from safe.

The potion or being there with Betty or having Avery there as a friend—something was giving him the strength to anticipate what was only yet being threatened. As immobile as he felt, he knew he was being protected by a force that... knew him. It was such a strange feeling. Womblike. Surprisingly like the sense he always had out on the moors, away from his fellow man, surrounded by the sheer starkness of Nature.

The sizzling hiss of high-voltage electrical energy crackled across the room with a growing insistence as the small table became the centre of a vortex of what felt more like emotion than any other force. Avery felt a tightening around his heart that had him clutching at his chest with the desperation of a child. Or a dying man.

Damien sensed the agony but could do nothing. As death approached his friend, his mind was drawn elsewhere, to the cold depths of the pub's freezer behind the bar. The image of Charlotte and Rufus, grey as stone, motionless, expectant, cut through the atmosphere that now was singed by green strobes of light. Rooted to his seat, Damien found the challenge of caring for his friend countered by a sudden concern for two apparent corpses he knew nothing about.

Betty watched with cunning insight. Nodding to the barkeep, she kept her gaze fixed on Damien, squinting with a concentration that brought her close to exhaustion. Fiona put a hand on Avery's shoulder as she saw him begin to convulse but quickly withdrew it at Betty's angered reaction. Not a word was spoken, not another gesture made, until the preserved bodies of the space travellers were rolled out on gurneys.

Giving off clouds of shimmering whiteness, the couple lay side by side nearest Betty, while a throbbing sound pulsed across the pub and co-ordinated with the beating of Damien's heart. There was no mistaking his choice. It was his friend or these two strangers. Bring life, take life. Save one, save two. Be human or transcend caring.

Beads of sweat rolled down Damien's face as he sat in agonizing in-decision, just able to see out of the corner of his eye the crippling attack his friend was suffering and the two bodies that were fast thawing nearby. A wicked howl of laughter sounded out of the electric green haze that remained over their table. It sounded like the hiss of a snake coupled with the choking laugh of a hyena. Pure malice. Pure nature. Pure perversion. Pure dread.

Slowly, movement returned to the young Englishman's face. A slight twitch animated the area around his eyes. A grimace formed, followed by a frown. He was being freed up to make his decision. He had to commit, he had to decide, he had to show his true colours. And yet he had no idea how this was to be. As an executioner, he had no previous experience. He had never even shot a grouse. And now he was expected to decide be-tween saving his friend and reviving two complete strangers, young as they seemed and presumably innocent. It was completely unfair, particularly since he knew how he was expected to act.

Saving a friend was as natural as breathing, after all. Saving two strang-ers was reduced to a matter of arithmetic, soulless and simplistic. And this, he knew instinctively, was just the beginning of his ordeal. His right hand twitched. It was indicating his friend, Avery. It was acting as the sceptre of fate in this duel for his mind and soul.

Convulsions and low moans escaped the two prone bodies. Betty waved a hand, and they were trundled back to the locker without ceremony.

Slowly, life returned to the group at Betty's table. Avery lost most of the purple/grey tone his face had turned to, and he began to breathe normally. Damien managed to squirm out of what had seemed like a death grip. His relief at seeing his friend revive was almost as palpable as the regret he felt at his decision not to save the two strangers. There was no way he could possibly express his angst at his decision, but there was no way he would have made it any other way. He suddenly realized he had been so compromised by what he had done that he now was stripped of any innocence that might have served him well in what might be his future challenges. He gave Betty a pained look of regret, which she returned with a knowing grimace and wink.

"You will need our help now more than ever," she whispered. "They have your measure now, and I am not sure it is what we need." She spat. "They will be using your weakness in the future, your flawed support of an old man over two young lovers. They will know you are no more than human and act accordingly."

"And what if I had acted differently?" Damien felt a surge of indignation course through his still-numbed body. "How did I know those two were young lovers? And of what ethical value, especially set against my friend, who I know to be wise and good?" His blood began to flow again. "How can I be judged lacking in a case like that?"

Betty flinched. "We shall see, your lordship. We can only wait now and see what judgment you have drawn." She shook her head. "If only I had my Euripides to guide me, I would feel so much less vulnerable…"

"Euripides, your cat?" Damien felt a jolt of electricity course through his body. It had the odd effect of both stimulating and emptying his mind. "Your…familiar, of course."

Betty just eyed Damien with ever more hopeful glances. "You have information? You know something about my beloved cat?"

"I know that it is not your beloved cat," Damien found himself saying, much to his surprise.

Betty appeared to shrink noticeably and let out a low cry. "How dare you say that" was all she managed, shaking with rage.

Damien let out a curse. "He is—how do you say?—an avatar, of course. Why I know this is quite beyond me." He looked most uncomfortable. "Something has happened—that cursed drink you ordered for us—that is turning me into…I feel as though I have been held up by highwaymen, stripped of any defences, vulnerable as a little girl." He put both hands to his head. "What on earth is happening?"

Betty turned to Avery, who was aghast at the entire scene. "You will need to look after your friend, Professor. He has chosen a path that may lead to quicker destruction than even I thought might be likely. He needs your support, your…caring."

Avery nodded. "We all need that, don't you think, Mistress Betty?"

CHAPTER NINETEEN

"**T**wo bodies? At the What and What?" Inspector Graham had had a full-enough day without this intrusion.

"The Goat and Dragon, Inspector." Leftenant Forsythe raised her eyebrows sceptically. "I've never heard of it myself. Somewhere off Mean Street, I suspect."

"Very amusing, Sandy. Just what I need at this stage in my life—a nonexistent pub with two corpses and no possible leads. I swear, that whole thing about the end of the world would have made life a lot easier, if you ask me."

"Begging your pardon, sir, but there are some of us who might like to have another night out before the great curtain comes down, you know."

Graham cast an appreciative eye on his aide. "Well, if I were your age...Yes, I see your point, Leftenant. Work has its rewards, but play has them, too. Of course, I do forget."

"And it was that nice Professor Owens who reported them. It's not as though they were just lying in a dark alley, overrun by rats."

"Yes, yes, all right. Send two of our newest recruits after this wild-goose chase. It will be good training for the lads. We'll see what comes of it all, if anything can materialize from whole cloth, as this caper appears to be."

"As you wish, sir."

"Oh, and get young Derwentwater on the phone, would you? I understand he had something to do with this business, and I need to speak to him on a raft of other issues as well." Graham reached for his pipe and promptly forgot what he had planned to do next. "Blast! Wither the whippoorwill when the wind is in the willows, eh, Leftenant?"

"Um, right, sir. Wither, indeed." Sandy looked down at her iPad, which was blinking forlornly as a useless trinket at the moment. "I'll get Gallagher and Mason on the case. They could use a little education on the basics, as far as I can tell." She rubbed her backside thoughtfully.

"You don't mean to tell me that they have been taking liberties with your…person, Leftenant?" Graham jammed his pipe in his mouth and winced from the pain.

"Nothing I can't handle, thank you, sir." She straightened her tunic and slipped back through the inspector's outer door.

At the same moment, Graham's nose went haywire. He began to sneeze, to cough, and to have trouble breathing. He reached out toward the door that Forsythe had just exited but caught himself falling away from any nearby prop. A knee hit the carpeted floor with such force that he couldn't suppress a cry of pain. Thankfully, no one had heard. He knelt there in the middle of his office, giddy, hurt, and more than a bit afraid. After several moments of trying to orient himself, he reached for a nearby chair and dragged himself upright. Struggling to breathe evenly and see clearly, he was suddenly aware that there was something else in the room with him, a silent witness to his distress. "Sandy," he murmured incredulously, "is that you?"

A low snarl sounded from behind his desk, followed by a doleful yowl. He shook his head, certain he was imagining things he had no wish for. Slowly he made his way to where he could see his chair and its immediate surround. Under it, all but invisibly blending in with the grey of the carpet was a great, agitated, angry cat. As their eyes met, the animal gave off a loud hissing sound and laid its ears back menacingly. Graham managed to stuff his unlit pipe in his pocket and just stare at the creature that had appeared from what had to be his own state of mental breakdown.

"You're that damned cat," he managed, trying to keep calm and remotely sane. He knew from the pain in his knee that he wasn't dreaming. He managed to take in the entirety of his office: the books, the ashtray, the boring diplomas and obligatory photographs on the wall. There was nothing that helped him determine that he had lost it all. Nothing but the same beast that had materialized in his flat what seemed like an age ago.

His hand slowly worked its way to the buzzer on top of his desk. Why he felt so intimidated by a bloody cat was beyond him, but his vague memory of the other encounter with it brought back odd sensations. It had just appeared out of presumed thin air and taken off like a shot rabbit when Betty of Bournemouth came to the door. That much he could remember. Oh, God, yes. Then there was the spontaneous combustion of his pipe. Sandy had been there. They had both witnessed, almost, the improbable mind-over-matter trick he had been trying to pull off since his school days.

At least, that was his hope and supposition. But now that this cat had reappeared under equally mysterious circumstances, he had no idea what to think. If, indeed, his mind was any longer capable of rational thought. He fought the impulse to kick at the cat as he limped his way to his chair and fell into it with an exhausted grunt. Euripides skulked into a corner, hissing like a Komodo dragon.

"Leftenant, we have a problem," he said as Sandy's head poked in, responding to his call.

"Sir?" She immediately began to sniffle.

Graham nodded his head toward the noisy corner. "We have company. Quite uninvited."

Sandy did a double take. "Why, that's quite impossible, sir. Animals are not allowed here in the offices at any time." She peered at the crouching figure. "Why, that looks like that...how did it ever...?" She shook her head, as much to try and clear it as to register disbelief. "This can't be happening, sir."

"Brilliant deduction, Leftenant. Now, if you can just find a way to clear the animal out of here as readily as it appeared, I would be most grateful."

Raised eyebrows, more sniffles, and some heavy breathing followed as she stood by the door, totally uncertain as to what to do. "Funny." She reached for a kerchief. "I have never been allergic to cats before, but this one is driving me bonkers at ten paces."

"You too? Thank God. I was afraid I might be the only one. You are seeing what I see?"

"Of course, sir." She now scrutinized her boss. "The dear thing is quite real, as far as I can determine. Quite annoyed, it would seem. And not a mirage."

"Do you think you could manage to do something about the bloody thing, then, since you have determined that it is not a mental hiccup or a simple spell or anything but a wayward rodent killer?" Graham began to get his bearings back, though he remained seated.

"Right away, sir." She leaned forward tentatively. "Here, kitty, kitty."

With a loud snarl, Euripides clawed at Sandy's outstretched hand, missing by millimetres. Quickly recoiling, Sandy stood as she backed up. "I suggest that we call the owner of this creature, sir, if we are likely to rid ourselves of it without bloodshed."

"Good idea, Leftenant. Do get on with it, would you? I suspect you may have to call Owens to find out where that old witch is living these days." He paused briefly, pondering what he had just said. "I suspect I can conduct business from your desk until this matter is resolved, what?"

"As you say, sir."

* * *

Betty nearly fainted at the news. "My Euripides! My life, my spirit, is back? They have relented and released him unhurt? Oh, savage day!"

Avery had no adequate response to that reaction to his phone call. He could only repeat the inspector's address and the request that she stop by at her earliest convenience. He found himself talking to a dead line since she had dashed for the door, Fiona and Missy in close pursuit. In their excitement, they hailed a cab, an expense that seldom entered any of their thoughts. When Scotland Yard was given as the destination, the deep scepticism of the cabbie was as silent as the tomb.

"A spot of bother, have we, ladies?" Curiosity overcame his customary restraint.

"I'll bother your spot if you don't minds your own beeswax, young man." Betty was in a euphoric mood, or there would have been an explosion of invective instead of such a tame exchange.

"Right you are, ma'm." The poor cabbie took longer than he might have studying his fare in the rear-view mirror and nearly hit a pedestrian at a crosswalk. "Beggin' your pardon, ma'm, but how do you do that?"

"Do what, you foolish man?" Betty leaned forward and was about to lose her temper.

"Why, not show yourself, of course. All I can make out is a glimmer where your eyes should be—in the mirror, that is. There's no face, no nothing else." He tried to keep his eyes on the road but couldn't.

"Oh, that's just my makeup, you miserable fool." Betty preened herself with a sneer. "It's the latest thing, if you must know. 'Invisible Wrinkles,' it's called. Now watch where you're driving. We needs to get where we're going, you got it?"

"Yes, ma'm. Got it." With a growing frown of confusion, the driver dodged several other near misses and came to a dramatic halt in front of the busy entrance to Britain's hub of police detection. As the three poured out, spluttering at the cost of the ride, the cabbie muttered something about broomsticks being cheaper that fortunately went unheard.

"That's one good reason not to take cabs," Betty remarked as they presented themselves at the visitors' desk inside. In response to the enquiring glances from her companions, she simple replied, "Mirrors."

It was at that moment that she took a sudden deep breath. "Oh, horrors. That could be what this is all about." Growing all but frantic, she obviously put off the young woman processing her request to see Inspector Graham. Missy and Fiona were in the dark as to what she might have meant but shared her sense of urgency that further slowed down the process of gaining access to the Yard's inner sanctum. "All we're here for is me cat what somehow got lost and found its way to the inspector's offices, you know?" Betty fixed the young lady at the desk with a firm look and a slight toss of the head. "We're here to do a service for the inspector, we are. A little house cleaning, you might call it."

Her anxiety grew at every moment. Something was terribly wrong. There was no reason for Euripides to reappear where he did, none whatsoever. There was little reason for him to reappear anywhere. Standing there in the middle of the daily hubbub of London's nerve centre of police action, Betty suddenly realized the fallibility of it all. Looking around suspiciously, she was about to abandon the whole idea of saving her cat. It had to be some sort of trap, some sort of ruse, some sort of treachery.

A hint of thunder sounded from some nearby source, causing several heads to turn and check that the sun was, indeed, still shining. A number of iPads appeared as the weather was checked. Puzzled faces stared at the screens that stated the all clear for the area. No showers, no clouds even, much less thunder storms. The harried young desk clerk finally got through to Sandy's phone and received the order to let Betty proceed to the inspector's office. She would require no escort but was asked to come along alone.

Stepping into the elevator with a flurry of agitation, she was followed closely by a plainclothesman. "Going my way?" he said pleasantly enough.

"That all depends, now don't it?" The sense of entrapment couldn't have been much greater. At least there are no mirrors in this infernal contraption, she thought with little relief. As she eyed her companion, she felt the strain and worry drain from her mind. Could it be getting close to her beloved Euripides that was giving her this sense of security? Could it be a totally false sense that was somehow cast over her, like one of her own spells? The very absence of anxiety was unnatural, an obvious alert that came too late now as the elevator drew ever deeper into the bowels of an agency she should have been more wary of.

The frozen smile on the face that stared at her grew more bizarre by the moment. The man's eyes seemed glazed over, as though they were both made of glass. He didn't even smell right, she realized. An odd synthetic scent caught her attention. And it didn't come from his suit, which was of Scottish wool, as one might expect. Some idiotic new cologne, she thought briefly, wishfully.

There was nothing for her to do but get off at the designated floor and follow the directions to Graham's office. The man just followed a few steps behind. As she passed various offices, life inside them seemed reassuringly normal. Mostly gruffness, some laughter, controlled chaos. But as she advanced, a bubble seemed to form around her, and not a protective one. It felt more and more like a cave, a prison, a cell. And she had had to leave her staff downstairs. There was no protection from anything until she reached her cat. The great god Zeus knew how little that might matter now.

"Well, well, what a relief!" Inspector Graham all but threw his arms around Betty as she swept into his office. "That will do, Jones. Thank you." He nodded at the man who had followed Betty the whole way and waited for him to disappear back down the hallway. "Good man. A bit eager." He stepped back to indicate the infuriated form of Euripides. "You can never be sure about the Welsh, of course." In the same breath, he said,

"Behold your beast, madam. A bit worse for wear, I warrant, but intact, nonetheless."

He raised his hands in complete bafflement. "How he ever found his way here will remain one of the Yard's great mysteries, I fear." An attempt at a smile fell flat.

Betty tried to tell what might be different about the inspector, how he might have been altered by whatever force was now controlling events—as control them, she knew it did. His eyes, the window to so much more than just the soul, showed no dilation of the pupils, no glassy soullessness that she would have suspected from her sense of insecurity. If there were evil afoot here, of all places, it might want to be a bit more subtle.

In a single bound, Euripides was in Betty's grasp, all but knocking her over in its haste to be repatriated. With a mixture of relief and joy, she clutched her cat and winced at the same moment. A pain starting in her lower back seemed to spread like molten lava through her body. Unwilling to let her beloved cat go, she felt the pain spread rapidly, even though she knew it had to have been triggered by her holding Euripides.

"Sit, Mistress Betty. You look done in." The inspector motioned for Sandy to bring up a chair. "Fetch some water and a bit of brandy, just in case. The latter's for both of us, of course, just in case." This time a wan smile showed through.

As Betty sat, clinging all but childishly to her pet, the inspector circled around to take his place once more behind his desk. "Have you the first foggy notion of how that animal wound up here in my offices?"

Betty squinted and just shook her head. She peered around the room, trying to pick up hints as to what it might have been that had brought Euripides back. The timing was too good. She had allowed herself to become desperate, to become clumsy, careless. And like a wave that has risen out of the sea with singular fury, she realized the inspector was one of the few individuals she thought she could trust. She tried once more to detect some tell-tale tick of oddness about him. Nothing. That was the worst, she suddenly knew. Confirmation that the spirits were acting with greater guile than she had thought possible. If there were no visible signs of cosmic interference, no identifiable stamp of deceit, the end was less remote and more certain than she had thought.

Sandy brought water, which the old woman refused. All she wanted was to get out of that claustrophobic place with her cat. It no longer mattered if she perished, as long as she had her dear Euripides. But not there in the bowels of propriety, of Britain's presumed straight and narrow.

"I'd be grateful if you'd let me go, Inspector, me and my friend 'ere." She stroked the cat as it sat purring on her lap.

"Why, of course. You are both most free to go." Graham gestured gladly at his door.

Betty eyed the distance to the exit and wondered if they would allow her to get as far as that. The look on Sandy's face was one of odd concern, as though she might be contemplating just how to finish them both off. Without soiling the rug. Slowly, she rose, clutching her cat now so close that he let out a yowl of protest. Taking that as a sign of possible danger, she bolted for the door.

The next thing she knew, she was somehow downstairs at the front desk with Missy and Fiona making a great fuss over Euripides. Sandy and the inspector each had a shot of brandy and exchanged comments of extreme puzzlement before getting back to work.

CHAPTER TWENTY

"**T**hat old woman from Bournemouth wishes to speak with you, your lordship." Horace held the offending phone away from him as though it harboured the plague.

"Oh? I do hope she has found her bloody cat." Damien set down his glass of claret and the book on Pythagoras he was reading.

"I believe she has, sir. She appears to be quite exercised about its return and some sort of infestation. I couldn't quite make out of what, sir." Horace's nose rose for a tremulous moment. "Fleas, I suspect."

"Now, now. We must refrain from supposition, my dear man, and assume the best at all times." Damien ignored the frown that that elicited.

"'Twas ever so, sir." The devoted servant stepped reluctantly forward with the iPhone in hand.

Minutes later, Damien was dressed and out the door. If ever there was a wild-goose chase he had no interest in, it was this one, but the sense of urgency in Betty's voice had compelled him to contact Avery as he set out to find the Goat and Dragon one last time. Thoughts of demons somehow didn't plague him, in spite of what Betty seemed to imply with her incoherent ramblings. His own sanity was what drove him now to do whatever he could to get through the next few hours. That iconic phrase of the rat race, "Time is of the essence," seemed to mock him as he sat trembling in the back of the cab that raced through the late evening streets to an unknown destination.

The cabbie knew there was no such pub anywhere in greater London. But the promise of a fifty-pound tip had him careening around corners as though they were caught up in a Grand Prix race. He even resorted to something that would have the entire city gawking. He stopped to ask the way, something that went against the grain of centuries of custom. Finally, sensing the need to get out and walk those fateful final blocks, Damien had the cab pull over. Exhausted by frustration, he set out feeling more like a bat than anything else, flying blind.

The neighbourhood looked familiar, particularly as it darkened under flickering gas lamps. The few individuals on the street kept to the shadows, hiding their faces and moving silently. No sooner had his thoughts wandered to the foggy lots of prewar films than a familiar voice sounded through the darkness.

"I say, is that you, Derwentwater? Have I found a friend in the midst of this misery?" Avery's voice sounded oddly disjointed, a trick of the night air, no doubt.

Turning to confront the dark figure advancing through the shadows, Damien extended a gloved hand and let out a sigh of great relief. "Old friend, we are well met, indeed, if we are in time to deal with whatever it is that Betty has in store for us."

"And if we can find that confounded pub of hers. Wouldn't you know that we have to wander aimlessly for God knows how long before it shows itself." Avery shivered. "Deuced difficult."

"All I can remember about finding it is that it shows up when and how it chooses, so there is nothing for us to do but continue to wander, what?" Damien tried to comfort himself with a good look at his friend's face, but the lighting wouldn't oblige. "Tell me, what do you imagine she has found out? What new horrors must we hope to endure before the Dark Ones act, before the End of Days?"

"If I knew the answer to that one, old man, I might consider retiring to the Riviera before it's too late." Avery's hand rested gently on Damien's shoulder.

"Yes, we might all consider such an inspired move, if there was any promise that the Riviera would be there when we arrived."

"Always presuming that there would be a means to get there, of course. One has to be practical about such matters, I should think." Avery's voice sounded increasingly distant. Another trick of the night air and the winding street, no doubt. A wistfulness mingled with a sense of loss. "There! There, I see a light." The two of them hurried forward and entered the pub, all but paralyzed by dread. At her usual table toward the back, they could make out the dwindled form of the one who had summoned them.

The usual silence fell upon their entrance into the dimly lit hall that harboured the usual suspects. Betty barely looked up from petting her cat as they approached her. "You have done well to find us, gents. At least there is that to celebrate. We have the power yet to draw you into our merry little band." She squinted at the two who stood waiting to be asked to sit. "I fear that, even with my precious Euripides returned to me, there may be little more to our influence any longer."

"That sounds like the jaws of defeat right there," Damien noted ruefully, "but as we did manage to find you, there must be a bit of magic left in the old lantern, don't you think?"

"Thinking is for others and at another time," Betty retorted. "We are at a critical moment that requires action, not words; deeds, not contemplation. And yet we are powerless…unless there is some way that we can harness your energy, your…innocence, your lordship."

"My innocence, if ever I suffered such a condition, is long gone, as you know, ma'am." Damien nodded toward the locker, where the two lovers had been stored.

"Ah, yes. That little incident." Betty concentrated on petting her cat. "Sad, indeed, for the pair who lost. But not an entire waste of effort." She looked up to scrutinize Damien's puzzled features. "You saved your friend here, and that was an act of what Christians call redemption." She rocked forward in her chair. "You displayed the common human frailty of compassion, caring more for someone you knew than for two strangers. 'No fault,' as they say in the *I Ching*." She suppressed a smirk. "Your weakness was apparently regarded as a strength by those who chose to judge. There must be some room yet for saints where we are all bound to go."

The sound of the front door being rattled drew everyone's attention. The outline of Willy, silhouetted against the dark night, swayed as he tried in vain to come in off the street.

"Will someone let that bumbling fool in?" Betty turned to spit, then raised a hand in caution. "Wait, wait!" She closed her eyes in communion with some far-off voice. "It's too late. Leave the poor illegitimate spawn of mindless debauchery to his fate." She gazed with a detached glaze in her eye that gave the others chills. "It is long as it should have been…" With only the slightest tick of conscience, she watched her son begin to pound at the glass door that wouldn't yield to his every more desperate effort to find haven.

Damien could not bear to watch. "Why can he not enter? What has he done? Why does the door not open?"

Betty looked up with a frigid resolve. "You are yet too human, young man. Your imagination is still mired in the swamp of fools, I see." She turned to gaze once more at the frantic figure of her son. Euripides looked up and snarled a cold message of doom, just as Willy collapsed in a heap. "At last," she managed in a choked whisper.

Avery made an attempt to rush to the door but found himself rooted to the spot. Everyone there had remained frozen in place. Heads had swivelled, but not a muscle had been flexed to try to save Willy. There was no trace of emotion anywhere in the pub, except the obscene absence of caring, a vacuum that Nature should have abhorred.

For the first time, Damien began to realize just what dimension he and Avery had been drawn into. He could feel the sweat forming at the back of his neck, even as his mouth went dry and breathing became an effort. He could see that his friend was suffering a similar reaction, only far more pronounced. With a hand once more clutching his chest, Avery had grasped the back of a chair and slowly lowered himself to what he hoped was a safe state of rest.

Damien tried to fix his gaze on Betty, thinking she might give him a focal point of reason or at least a means to help keep his wits about him. She looked up with all the bitterness that an old crone might have conjured in the Dark Ages.

"Now you are part of our world, Mr. Lordship. Now you are a lost soul, as are we. Now you can taste of the sorrow and waste and wanton destruction of this world that your kind has visited on the planet all this time." She paused only to spit. "Now you know why there is no tomorrow for any of us, thanks to your kind."

"I know only that you are a heartless, cruel creature, seemingly beyond all redemption. That is all I know from what I have seen." Damien gazed around the room and saw not a pair of eyes that would meet his.

Betty snorted in disgust. "One death and you are an imperious judge of all life, Master Damien? I would have thought that you would have learned by now." She leaned forward in apparent pain. "I had hoped, like a fool, that you might see more clearly than that."

Avery struggled to speak. "For God's sake, man, lighten up." His features suddenly began to relax. The pain in his face smoothed into a benign calm. "Yes, just lighten up, old man. There's only one way out of this, you know." He leaned back and looked for all the world as though he were listening to Mozart. A slight lilt to his right hand directed the imaginary orchestra.

Betty watched this development with keen interest. Her fingers twitched and twisted as she waited to see what might happen next. Every so often she would stare at the crumpled heap of her son's body outside the door, and a frown would scour her face. And then she would look away, with no trace of guilt or remorse. Damien watched with increasing fascination and dread. There was a slender thread of hope that separated him from what seemed like the dull certainty of doom that Betty shared with her kind. Knowing that he and Avery alone might hold what felt like the future of the world in their hands did nothing for his nerves, much less his stomach. A knot grew tighter by the minute as he contemplated the idiocy of trying to second-guess Fate, to fool the Dark Ones into giving them all another chance.

What was it that Avery had said so long ago now about the possible vulnerability of the invisible, undetectable force that now seemed poised to obliterate all of creation? Something about the outrage brought on by humanity's inhumanity, a need for chastisement for all the wanton destruction to the harmonic fibre of the universe. Judgment, in a word, for all the random acts of madness and greed that have plagued Mankind throughout history. But—here was the crux—remaining sceptical about it all. It seemed too simple, too logical, far too pat.

He tried to decipher what Avery was going through. Where was the agony of the End of Times? Why did this seem as empty of threat as the Mayan calendar theory? Why did his every sense tell him he was trapped in a world that was unchanged by physical, spiritual or psychological disruption? He managed to read the expressions on Missy and Fiona's faces for the first time. Absolute calm, mirroring Avery's. Nothing made sense until everything made sense. He had been lured into a world of mindless destruction and mystery and misery, and but for the door that wouldn't open for Willy, it was identical to any reality he knew of. The only difference seemed to be in measure, in intensity, in a euphoric feeling of guileless innocence. Whatever happened in this world, in this tiny realm, was free of guilt because it was the exact replica of a world dictated by human failures, foibles, and fantasies. But the inhabitants were not human.

Betty gave a knowing nod at what she determined Damien had discovered. "Through the rabbit hole, eh, Master Damien? Not too much pixie dust for you, is there?" She cackled, slapped her knee, and then motioned to Fiona. "Tell him, dearie, just where we really are, where the chickens come home to roost."

The young woman's face lit up as she licked her lips and adopted a far-off look. "When I was really young, some three hundred years ago, we all huddled in fear and poverty and filth. The simple fact was that our number and influence was nothing in the face of murderous bigots and mindless fools." She actually smiled at the memory of it all. "We paid for our independent thought with persecution and death. We were the vagabonds of society, the outcasts, the targets of convenience." She turned unseeing eyes toward Avery. "Your fellow traveller, Galileo Galilei, joined our ranks as a blasphemer and iconoclast until he grovelled before the Inquisition in order to save his life. Those were times when we paid dearly for our beliefs, our understanding of the makings of the universe."

Missy couldn't resist joining in. "Fear of all the vast unknown gave rise to hatred and deceit even then, Professor, as you well know, in far greater measure than you have had to face in your own lifetime."

Avery's smile broadened even as he nodded in complete understanding. He said not a word, however, and continued to conduct his imaginary orchestra.

"So," Damien concluded, "the persecuted become the persecutors. Is that it?"

Betty convulsed at that statement. "Lordy, no, you idiot." She couldn't keep herself quiet now. "Don't tell me that you are going to make my son look intelligent by comparison. What Fiona has tried to make clear is that our kind suffered the indignities of the weak, the outcasts of society, even when we had powers of conviction and knowledge." She paused to spit. "It has now come to pass that we are the ones, allied with what you call the Dark Ones, who hold the cards, as it were."

"I believe I get that, Mistress Betty, but where does that leave any of us?" Damien waved his hands in the air. "You have acted as though all hell was about to break loose, that we all were doomed, that the entire human race was about to pay big-time for our history of folly." He paused to consider what he had just said. He saw the sly look on Betty's face. He really didn't need to know more.

"It is just that simple, your lordship. We all are about to pay for your folly. We, the keepers of the flame, the ones who have known and cared for all Creation, are being threatened as much as all of your kind who deserve the rage and oblivion that Nature promises."

Damien shook his head. There was something he knew he was supposed to understand, yet could not. There was the something he had felt at Stonehenge, which now tugged at the primitive recesses of his brain. Now, daring not to look at Betty or her cohorts and embarrassed to see even if Avery was all right, he stiffened with the impact of his sudden revelation. He was, or at least felt, invincible. There was a dreamy chorus that chanted, much like ancient monastic voices, that he was unique, that he alone could survive the test of fire that was about to be let loose.

He managed to focus on Betty once more. She was squinting with the agony of a mother giving birth. And he was the baby, the by-product of immense effort and pain and sacrifice. Fiona and Missy were the midwives, attendant, dutiful, there. Even Avery's far-off look of bliss seemed now to fit the scene. All hope of survival now seemed to be on his shoulders. But only if he could convince the Dark Ones that he was their target. That was the crux of it all. He now knew what he had to be, if not do. But how to determine that he was the Chosen One? How could he convince all who wanted Mankind to perish that he was the agent through whom to make it so? How could he hope to survive the ravages of being targeted, even as invincible as he then felt?

Euripides seemed to supply an answer when he arched his back and dug his claws deep into Betty's legs. Pinpoints of red dotted Betty's skirt even as she howled in agony and tossed him to the floor. Cursing profusely, she kicked at the cat, even as it leaped into Damien's lap. A gasp sounded at this sight, with worried murmurs all around the pub.

Betty's cry of pain lowered into a moan of loss and sadness, while Fiona and Missy nearly collapsed from sheer disbelief. Damien was caught so much by surprise that he found himself petting the cat instinctively. The sounds of purring were immediately hypnotic.

Avery managed to pull himself out of his state of reverie to take in this unexpected scene. "That a boy. That a boy." He eyed both cat and man, and you couldn't tell which he might be talking to.

CHAPTER TWENTY-ONE

Inspector Graham gently set down his mug of coffee and reached for the intercom. "Sandy, would you come in, please. I…need you for a moment." The door flew open at this unprecedented request. and the leftenant stood poised for action.

"Beg pardon, sir. Is everything all right?"

"I'm not at all certain, young lady." Graham felt horribly under-whelmed. "Just a gut feeling thus far, but that pipe of mine just lit itself up—quite by itself, mind you—and my head feels like a belfry chock-full of bats." He put one hand to his forehead and felt like a pathetic silent-screen star.

"Really, sir?" Sandy stiffened her back, ready for anything. "Now, if that cat shows up, we'll know for certain that something is rotten in the state of Denmark."

"Won't we now!" The inspector couldn't resist a quick check in the corners for the cat. With a self-deprecating grunt he attempted an embar-rassed smile followed by a deep frown. "There's something rotten, all right, but it isn't in Denmark." He shook his head, befuddled. "If I only knew where…and even what, I could feel as though I am getting somewhere, if that makes any sense."

"I believe that the very lack of coherence in that statement, sir, says it all." Sandy shot a worried look at her boss and wished she had a clue as to what to do.

"Tell me this, Leftenant." Graham sighed as he sat uncomfortably in his swivel chair. "If you were my age...no." He scratched his forehead. "That does not compute, as they say these days."

"What does not, sir?"

"Why, the most basic measures of communication, of course. Everything, from simple diction to subatomic particles to God knows what! Google, Wikiponder, *Star Wars*. All that rubbish."

"Wikipedia, do you mean, sir?"

Graham fixed his aide with a worried stare. "I haven't the foggiest, Sandy. That's my point. I have no idea what any of this modern gobbledygook means, much less do I care a hoot. Damn, where was that asteroid when I needed it most?"

"They are out there, sir. Thousands of them, from what I hear. And they periodically do sneak through our defences, if defences we have, and come whizzing close enough to give us a good tan, even at our..."

Graham feigned a smile. "I am well aware of that much astronomy, thank you, Leftenant. It was just hopeless selfishness on my part that would have appreciated a swift end to all this mindless discomfort we call life." He sighed deeply.

Sandy's eyebrows rose several degrees over her startled features. "Surely you don't mean that, sir. Why...just because you're approaching retirement...and perhaps not feeling as chipper as you once did...that's a terrible thing to wish on the rest of us poor minions of Fate who would like to see a few more sunsets..."

"Yes, yes. I apologize. We have had this discussion before, I now remember. It's just that there is something eating at my gut that I can't begin to understand. And then there is my pipe. Look at the damned thing! Sending smoke signals from the next world. Can you believe?"

Sandy leaned forward at that comment to verify what she had just heard. "Good Lord! No. That's just what it looks like to an untrained eye." She shook her head stubbornly. "That's a figment of your imagination, Inspector. Believe me! Smoke signals!" Her eyes bulged as she spoke. Puffs of grey cloud rose and dispersed, just as she had seen as a child in the movies.

"A figment of my what, Leftenant?" Graham stared bleakly at the pipe.

"There has to be some explanation, sir." Sandy's face began to twitch as she searched the room for some plausible clue as to why they both seemed to be going mad. "Begging your pardon, sir, but what had your findings told you about spontaneous combustion? Those studies you made when you were a student?"

"Oh, those? Hah! That was so long ago. Almost when the world was young, it seems now." Graham picked up his pipe and stuck it possessively between his teeth. With a far-off look, he recited his findings. "'There is a time when thought may become matter, when perception is indivisible within the sphere of the experience of being. It has been proven throughout history that physical elements can be manipulated through the power of thought (or prayer/meditation) almost at will.'" He came out of his reverie with a broad smile now on his face. "'When the mind chooses to manifest itself as matter, it may do so by any number of means, including through incantation, dance, chemical means, even simple suggestion.'" He pointed an accusatory finger. "Is that what you were after, you crafty, young thing?"

"I had no idea, really. I just knew that you would have some explanation for all this smoke and mystery, with or without mirrors." She shrugged, relieved yet still uncertain.

"Right you are. Mirrors? What…oh, yes. 'Smoke and mirrors.' Very clever. Of course. Where is my head these days?" Graham reached up to be sure there was something still sitting on his shoulders. A creaking sound came from the bookcase along the far wall. Then there was a distinct rumble and agitation everywhere. "Good Lord, an earthquake!" He instinctively grabbed hold of his desk, one of the few objects in the room that seemed unaffected.

Sandy managed to drop into a chair before she fell over from the persistent vibrations that were sending all sorts of articles tumbling like puppets with their strings cut. She clapped her hands to her ears as the grinding, snapping sounds of invisible hands toying with their lives threatened to drive her crazy. She let out a scream. It felt like the last remnant of control she might have over her environment. Then it all stopped. The ensuing silence was broken by cries of anguish and anger all over the Yard, but the heaviness of the aftermath was sullen and brooding. Everyone braced for aftershocks.

A junior officer rushed in to check on damage or injuries and was gone in an eager flash to be in as many places as possible. Graham fixed Sandy with a weary look. "I told you I had a gut feeling something was going to happen. I had no idea it was going to be like this, but I knew there had to be something destructive and...evil."

"We had better clear the building, sir, in case there are fires or wreckage or further collapse with renewed tremors." Sandy got to her feet and took a tentative step forward to help the inspector out of his chair. The sounds of sirens and loud voices barking orders mingled in the dusty aftermath of what proved to be the first category six earthquake ever recorded in the London area.

"Makes you wonder, doesn't it, Leftenant?" Graham gingerly stepped out into the hallway, where commotion reigned.

"About what, exactly, sir?"

"About my gut feelings, for one." He puffed out his chest. "I haven't been so right on about events for some time now. I used to have quite a knack...oh, never mind. Let's do as you suggest and get on out of here." He paused as he scanned the room with a pained sense of loss. "As soon as I check on my men, that is."

"Oh, I'm sure they can take care of themselves, sir." Sandy dodged a phalanx of younger men who were scouring the building, looking for any injured personnel. "Best we clear the decks and gather outside." She took the inspector firmly by the shoulder and led him to the stairwell. "Best to walk, I suspect, don't you?" She felt quite maternal as she acknowledged nods and brief comments from the swirling mass of individuals busily going about their duty with blind abandon.

"As you say, Leftenant. I put myself at your disposal." Graham quite gratefully took hold of Sandy's arm and wouldn't let go until they were safely clear of the building. Regaining a measure of control, he barked out a few orders that went ignored in the general melee that now formed in front of the venerable headquarters of Scotland Yard. The relatively new structure showed no visible signs of destruction, beyond several shattered windows and loosened pediments that had already smashed into the surrounding sidewalks with no apparent injuries to passersby.

"Wouldn't you know," he murmured wistfully. As chaos continued to appear the order of the moment, his own mind grew preternaturally clear. He took a step away from Sandy as he straightened up to his former martial stance. His years in the Royal Navy now seemed as though just yesterday. He even forgot the accumulated aches and pains of recent years as he surveyed the scene as though from the deck of HMS. *Victory*. Instinctively, he knew that worse things were in store for all of them. Listening to reports that were coming in from all over the city, he knew that many of the older buildings were in ruins, their inhabitants dead or worse.

"Time's a wasting, Leftenant. Come with me." He arched an eyebrow, and a startled Sandy fell in behind him as they made their way to an undamaged patrol car. "Hop in. We're going to find that bloody woman who is behind all this."

"What bloody woman is that, sir?"

Graham took the wheel and felt like a colt as he accelerated away from the startled crowd outside the Yard. "Why, the witch from Bournemouth, of course. Who else is there under suspicion in this case?"

"I had no idea that there was any one person, sir. And certainly not an old hag with delusions of grandeur plaguing her every thought."

"Delusions, you say?" Graham shifted gears with a youthful intensity.

"Why, she seemed quite mad to me, sir." Sandy gripped the car door to steady herself as best she could as they careened through the dazed scene on every street. "Shouldn't you be a bit more cautious, sir? There is no power for stoplights, no personnel for traffic control, and no...Watch out!"

A group of elderly patients was pouring out of their retirement home, herded by a distracted pair of nurses. "Oh, Lord." Graham winced as he yanked at the steering wheel and hoped he wouldn't slide sideways into the crowd. The tyres screamed their protest. Frightened faces turned to stare. At the last moment the car righted itself and sped on by the bewildered and angry lot.

Sandy sat paralysed in her seat, unable to do more than shake her head. Cringing at the recklessness of Graham's driving, she finally ventured to note: "At this rate, Inspector, there will be nothing left of us as actors upon the stage." Her voice rose several octaves. "You have to slow down, or we will wind up in a heap...a wreck, a mangled mass of molten nothingness."

Graham frowned and glanced briefly at his aide. "Bloody hell!" He throttled back. "I suspect you're right. Of course." He wiped the sweat off his brow. "What was I thinking?" He dodged another mass of humanity as they swept out onto Trafalgar Square before cutting up Charing Cross

Road. "That damned pub is up this way somewhere. Help me keep an eye out, will you?"

"Of course. Of course. The name again?"

"The Goat and Dragon, as I remember. It's in an odd part of town. Owens told me all about it. God knows it may have been demolished by all this, too. It's apparently old enough to have witnessed the Norman invasion."

"I suspect Betty of Bournemouth would have us believe she witnessed the invasion herself, you know?" Sandy managed a smile as the inspector was driving now with some measure of care. This part of the city seemed oddly unaffected by the earthquake.

Graham gave that a moment's thought. "I suspect that from what I have heard, you're absolutely right." His frown deepened. "And that means one of two things. Either she is as batty as a fruitcake, or we could all be in for a rude awakening."

Sandy peered right and left and threw up her hands. "There just is no more sense to all this than Professor Owens's theory of dark matter, it seems to me."

Graham let out a loud guffaw. "My dear child, then how do you explain this horrible happening that has gutted a good bit of the city, not to mention that mysterious explosion of Betty's building, not to mention the case of the bloody cat that keeps on appearing, unbidden, and my pipe going off like Vesuvius, unlit?"

"Happenstance?"

"Humph. Most amusing. Ah, there we are. The Goat and Bloody Dragon. Look. Untouched! How do you explain that?" He set the parking brake with the energy of a young man and all but leapt from the car. "You'd best wait here. If I'm right about any of this…Damn, I shouldn't have brought you along."

"If you are remotely right about all this, you might need me more than either of us would like to admit." Sandy climbed firmly from her seat and stood poised by the bonnet, eyeing the pub. "Looks innocent enough, doesn't it? But then again, so did Auschwitz, I suspect, from a distance."

Graham made no comment, only squared his shoulders and advanced toward the pub's entrance. "This could get a bit rough. I do wish I had left you at the Yard."

"There was no more chance of that than my flying to the moon," Sandy replied, trailing close behind the slowly advancing inspector. "Yes, the more I think about it, the more this whole business smacks of some fantastic physical impossibility. Like the Higgs boson."

Graham paused briefly to look back. "The Higgs what?"

"That dimmed elusive particle that people have been spending billions to prove exists at some ridiculous subatomic level." Sandy's voice dropped as they approached the door, sounding conspiratorial. "They say it makes all else possible, by dint of not being part of anything else. Is that ridiculous, or what? It sounds just like all that blather about dark matter, doesn't it?"

Inspector Graham stopped in his tracks, turned, and frowned down at his subordinate. "Good Lord, woman, are you trying to tell me that this theory of dark matter is just a variation on some subatomic principle?"

"No, sir. Just that they sound suspiciously similar and painfully oblique." Sandy threw up her hands in frustration.

Graham could see into the pub from where he had stopped. Peering first at Sandy then quickly at the interior of the well-lit room, he muttered repeatedly, "Subatomic...suspiciously...Good grief, woman, what can of worms have you opened?"

Sandy glanced at her empty hands. "I haven't been near a can opener in days, sir."

Graham shook his head, trying to clear it of cobwebs. "Do stop being so literal, would you, Leftenant?"

"Sorry, sir. Can't help it, sometimes. A woman's curse, sir."

"A woman's...? Look, there's Owens and young Derwentwater, there with the old battle-axe. Time to advance, Leftenant, with full colours flying."

Sandy suppressed any further comment as the inspector reached for the door and found it quick to open. "Evening all," he called out a bit too boisterously as they entered.

All faces turned to stare, mostly sullen and brooding. "Glad to see your part of town seems spared from much of the devastation of this damned quake." Glancing around as he advanced on Betty's table, he felt more confident than ever for no reason he could possibly understand. "Hello, chaps, Mistress Betty, ladies." He nodded all round and waited for Sandy to step up by his side. "How much time would you say we have?"

"For what, Inspector?" Betty peered up with a pained expression.

"Why, for the next earthquake, for one…or for a visitation from hell or the asteroid with earth's name on it." His eyebrows did a bit of a dance. "I could name quite a number of items, and that would not include any of the more imaginative lulus my young assistant here might come up with."

Betty glowered and slunk back in her chair. "Do you make light of the fate of your planet, Mr. Policeman? Do you think you have any say in the outcome of where devils tread?"

"I think I have as much say as you might, you old bag of wind." Graham had never spoken like this to anyone before. It took everyone by total surprise. He responded gently to Sandy's tug on his sleeve. "What is it, de…Leftenant? Have I left anything out?"

Sandy cleared her throat defensively. "Begging your pardon, sir, but we are in a hostile environment, and the manual makes it clear that bravado and anger are not the best situation management tools for the job." She looked around with a cautious glimmer of optimism. "These good people are doing their best to do what they can to keep our world from imploding…You mustn't be too harsh on them for trying." Her almond eyes rolled open to stare hypnotically at each person at the table in turn.

"After all, they are just doing what they are programmed to do."

"Whatever do you mean by that?" Graham turned to peer at Sandy with a sudden sense of dread.

She stood, transformed from a neatly attired subordinate to a strangely out-of-focus being that hovered slightly above the floor. Betty gasped and let out a wail. Avery found himself laughing uncontrollably, pointing like a child at this spectre as it dissolved into a cloud of darkness. Missy and Fiona stared, petrified. The entire room let out a low moan as it, too, dissolved into swirling dust before a flash of light as bright as a thousand suns melted the very idea of time.

Made in the USA
Charleston, SC
25 June 2013